Catnappers

Other Titles by Ann Pilling

The Empty Frame
Black Harvest
The Pit
The Witch of Lagg
The Beggar's Curse
Amber's Secret

The
Catnappers

Ann Pilling

Illustrated by Clare Mackie

Collins

An imprint of HarperCollins*Publishers*

for Vera, his first person singular
for Celia, who did not give up hope
and for Annie, whose cat it was

First published in Great Britain by Collins 2003
Collins is an imprint of HarperCollins*Publishers* Ltd,
77–85 Fulham Palace Road, Hammersmith, London W6 8JB

The HarperCollins website address is
www.**fire**and**water**.com

1 3 5 7 9 8 6 4 2

Text copyright © Ann Pilling 2003
Illustrations copyright © Clare Mackie 2003

The author and illustrator assert the moral right
to be identified as the author and illustrator of the work.

ISBN 0 00 713726 5

Printed and bound in England by
Clays Ltd, St Ives plc

And in after years, if you would blame

His sadness, he was used to say,

'It's dull in our town since my playmates left!'

Robert Browning

The Pied Piper of Hamelin

Chapter One

Once upon a time there were two old ladies. Their names were Kitty and Miss McGee. Kitty was tall and thin and liked to sit in a tall, thin chair. Miss McGee was little and round and preferred sitting on a plump, soft settee with puffy cushions. Kitty's real name was Katherine, but Miss McGee called her Kitty. Her own name was

Florence, but Kitty called her "McGee"; she only used Florence when she got cross with her, but this didn't happen very often. It was normally Miss McGee who got cross.

This was because Kitty was a bit vague and dreamy, and went round saying little poems to herself. Her pale, oval face, the exact shape of an egg, was so calm and quiet-seeming that looking into it was like looking into a deep, calm lake.

Kitty and Miss McGee were very old. When they were little girls, there were no televisions or computers or mobile phones. In those days, a cart came along pulled by a little horse, and a man threw the coal for your fire down a hole in the pavement. The streets were lit by pretty lamps, worked by gas, and every night, before the dusk came, another man came round with a long stick and switched them all on. He was called the lamplighter. "Remember the lamplighter, McGee?" Kitty would say dreamily, as they sat in their chairs after tea, watching the darkness fall. "Remember the coalman's horse?"

But you mustn't think that Kitty and Miss McGee were two fuddy duddies. It's true that they didn't have a television or a computer and their telephone was a very old-fashioned one. It was black and it weighed a ton and it had a loud, clanging bell. But they certainly kept up with things. They listened to the radio and they read the newspapers and they both kept a very sharp eye on what was going on in Golden Square, which was where they lived, at Number 19.

It was called "golden" because in spring the garden in the middle was full of daffodils. This garden was private with black railings all round, stuck with iron spikes, and you got inside by unlocking a gate. The old ladies had a key to it but they didn't go there much. It felt too lonely, sitting in the garden all by themselves.

Once there had been lots of families living in Golden Square. There had been a little school close by, too, and all the children used to play in the garden. They played hide-and-seek in the shrubbery, they climbed the trees and they skimmed pebbles across the small, round pond. But then the school had closed down and the families had all gone to live in new, shiny houses on the edge of the town. Apart from Number 19, all the houses in Golden Square had been turned into offices for dentists and doctors. In the evening everybody went home and there was silence.

"It's dull in our town since the children went," said Kitty to Miss McGee. "Even Debbie Springer seems to have deserted us. I really do miss Debbie."

Debbie Springer was a little girl whose mum did cleaning for some of the dentists and doctors who had offices in Golden Square. They used to live in a flat in the very bottom of one of the houses, but one day a water pipe burst and there was a flood. The water had turned the bottom of the house all dank and smelly and mould had begun to grow on the walls. But the man who owned it was a bit of a miser and wouldn't pay anybody to put the house right. So Mrs Springer, who had bright red hair and rather a hot temper, said "Right, then, we'll go and live somewhere else, somewhere nice and light and airy. You can keep your rotten old flat – we'll find another place!" And she had marched away with Debbie, refusing to pay the miser his last bit of rent: for which nobody blamed her one bit.

They soon found a new home and it was certainly airy. It was on the very top floor of the Town Flats. These looked a bit like skyscrapers and stood right in the middle of the town, quite dwarfing the Town Hall and the parish church. These were tall buildings but they looked tiny next to the Town Flats. To get to Debbie's flat you took a lift and whizzed up dozens of floors till you reached the very top. They didn't have a garden, of course, just a balcony full of plants, and nobody was allowed to have a cat or a dog, not living up there, almost in the sky. It wouldn't be fair. That was why Debbie had liked visiting the two old ladies who did have a pet.

They tried very hard to keep fit. Kitty tended their tiny garden, Miss McGee did the cooking and they both walked up and down the stairs a lot, because theirs was that sort of house. They also took little walks but they got tired more quickly than when they were young, and soon came home again.

"If only Nicholas could talk," Miss McGee said wistfully one day. "He takes very long walks: I expect he picks up all the gossip."

Nicholas was their cat and one of the reasons Debbie had liked visiting the old ladies, on the days when her mum dropped by to do a bit of cleaning for them. This hadn't happened very often as Mrs Springer had so many other cleaning jobs and needed the money. But she refused to take any from the old ladies because they were her friends and they only had their pensions.

Nicholas was very handsome. He was pale ginger, the colour of a lightly baked biscuit. His fur was soft and fluffy and his tail was fat and plume-like and rather resembled a feather duster.

"Who does your Nicholas belong to then?" said Mr Plackett the postman one day. He liked cats; they didn't snap at him like dogs did. Nicholas was not only handsome, he was also very friendly; he would talk to anybody.

"He's both of ours," explained Miss McGee. "We share him."

"But who owns the tail end?" said Mr Plackett. "That's the bit I'd like. I mean, you could dust all the cobwebs away with a tail like that. You could just tuck him under your arm, and get to work."

"Nobody owns it," Kitty told him rather coldly. She was alarmed at the idea of using

Nicholas's tail to clear cobwebs. "And nobody owns him. You can't own a cat. Nicholas belongs to himself alone."

"Don't get it," grunted Mr Plackett, walking off down the path. But Kitty wasn't listening. "The tail of Nicholas is the glory of God," she murmured. It was one of her poetry things.

It was certainly true that Nicholas was for ever going out, in fact, he was very sociable, and sometimes he did very bold things. Once, seeing a tasty-looking bird, he leaped from a first-floor window right down into the square, to try and catch it. He could have been squashed flat, but he wasn't. You probably know that a cat has nine lives. Well that day, Nicholas certainly lost one of them.

But there was one thing that always frightened him. If ever he heard a loud noise, he went pelting off to hide in some very secret place where he stayed for ages and ages – sometimes for hours.

It was because loud noises terrified Nicholas that everything went wrong, and it all started because of a silly quarrel. One day Miss McGee lost her temper with Kitty, and shouted and, rather to her surprise, dreamy Kitty shouted back. Then they threw things at each other and shouted more loudly, and it all made a very big noise indeed.

Kitty blamed Miss McGee and Miss McGee blamed Kitty and they both stormed off to sulk in their own rooms. But Nicholas didn't creep up the stairs to comfort them both, one by one, in his usual purry way, and this was because he had vanished.

But before we get on to that, there is something more pleasant to tell you, something quite exciting that happened in Golden Square, only days before the old ladies quarrelled.

Chapter Two

The excitement happened just a few weeks before Christmas. Miss McGee was busy, mixing her pudding. She normally made it on Bonfire Night so that it could sit for a good long time on the cool pantry shelf, and develop all its lovely flavours of fruit and spice and best brandy, and be just perfect for Christmas Day. But she had been ill in bed with a nasty cold so the pudding making had been delayed.

Kitty offered to make it for her. "I could do it, McGee," she said one morning, "if you will give me exact instructions."

But Miss McGee, who was still feeling rather ill, called out from her bedroom, "Oh no, thank you. When it comes to cooking, you're *hopeless*."

Poor Kitty crept away, feeling very crushed, and went to sit in her front room, quietly, among her plants, with Nicholas on her knee. "Dear McGee must be feeling very bad indeed," she confided, "or I don't think she would have said such a thing to her oldest friend, do you?" And while Nicholas purred, in an understanding kind of way (the old ladies told him all their troubles, both separately and together), a little tear trickled slowly down her cheek.

Kitty, who was not very good at forgetting hurtful things, such as being told she was "hopeless", was unhappy for the whole of that day, and into the next and the next. The unhappiness was like very bad toothache, just gnawing and gnawing, and it only went away when something unusual suddenly caught her eye, down in the square. It was a big, silvery furniture van with *Gentle Ghost Removals* painted on the side in bold blue letters.

"McGee," she called. "McGee, come quickly. Somebody's moving into Number 26." In spite of her creaky little legs, Miss McGee came up the stairs quite fast, to look for herself. People never moved *into* Golden Square, they always moved *out*.

For example, just as they had got used to little Debbie Springer running in and out of their house, calling them her "special grannies" (even though she had a perfectly nice gran of her own, who lived by the sea at Blackpool), the flood happened, and the green mould, so that, almost overnight, Debbie and her mum had gone. Much as Kitty and Miss McGee liked Debbie, they were both nervous about going to the top of the Town

Flats in that lift, so they didn't see her any more. And all this was part of the reason that the two old ladies, who loved families and pets and, most of all, children, felt lonely.

They stood side by side at the window and peered down into the square where three men in brown overalls were carrying things into the house. Kitty removed her spectacles, to see better, and Miss McGee put hers on, for the same reason.

"There goes the ironing board," Miss McGee cried. "And there goes the washing machine."

"And there goes a bicycle... no, *two* bicycles," said Kitty. "And they're quite little ones." She turned to her friend with shining eyes. "You don't suppose a real family's moving in, do you, McGee? Real people, after all those dentists and doctors? Might it be a real family at last, with real children?"

Miss McGee screwed her nose up, and her mouth and her eyes, till her face was one big scrunch. She didn't want Kitty to be disappointed, in case it wasn't a real family and she didn't want to be disappointed herself. They both liked children. Kitty had once been a teacher, in the school that had closed down. She had been used to little boys and girls playing round her feet all day. Miss McGee had been a special nurse and had cared for sick children in hospital. "I wouldn't like to say, Kitty," she replied. "It could be some young people moving in. They might keep us awake all night, with their noisy parties."

"Oh surely not," said Kitty (though secretly, she rather liked parties), "not in Golden Square."

The fetching and carrying went on for quite a long time, then there was a great slamming of doors. The driver whistled and soon the silvery van was moving away from the pavement. Just for an instant, the old ladies saw two grown-ups standing outside the door of Number 26, a man and a woman hand in hand. They were staring rather sadly at the disappearing removal van. Kitty and Miss McGee held their breath because the front door was still open; a handful of leftover autumn leaves was scurrying over the doormat.

"Where are the children?" whispered Kitty. "Perhaps they're inside, unpacking their toys. Perhaps, if we wait, they'll come out. They might even ride their bicycles round the square," and she pressed her nose against the window pane.

"I don't think so, dear," muttered Miss McGee and she hid her own disappointment by going back to the pudding making, down in her kitchen. "There probably aren't any children," she added, under her breath.

Chapter Three

Kitty decided that there had got to be children. Hadn't she seen two bicycles? So instead of doing her jobs, she spent a lot of time in her sitting room, lurking behind the curtains and peeping down into Golden Square. But nobody ever came out of Number 26.

Miss McGee got quite cross with her. It was now two whole days since they'd seen the removal van and all that time the pudding mixture had been soaking in a big, brown bowl, covered with a clean piece of cloth to keep out any flies or spiders. It was now time to boil it.

Kitty had funny feelings about this bowl because it was the very bowl that Miss McGee's grandfather, who had been a farmer, used to soak his poor tired feet in at the end of the day. The pudding was always delicious but each year, when she took her first mouthful at Christmas lunch, Kitty always thought of a pair of big, sweaty feet swishing about in the bowl it had been mixed in. But she never dared tell Miss McGee.

"Come along!" her friend called to her from the kitchen. "I've got the pudding ready, and it's time to start boiling. Stop mooning about by that window, Kitty, I need help."

"I'm not mooning," Kitty replied. "I've been waiting for those children to emerge from Number 26."

"I've told you, there are no children. Now put your finger on this knot for me, please. I want a really nice, tight top to the pudding."

Miss McGee had spooned her mixture out of the feet bowl into a white pudding basin. She had cut out a neat circle of greaseproof paper for the top then wrapped it all up in a big, special pudding cloth, the size of a tea towel. She had tied a string round this cloth, to keep it in place, and now, with the help of Kitty, it was secured with a very complicated knot.

The Christmas pudding, cocooned in its cloth, was quite heavy. Between them, Kitty and Miss McGee lowered it into a large saucepan which was ready waiting on the cooker. They filled the pan halfway up with water, then lit the gas. Five minutes later the water around the pudding was boiling fast and Miss McGee turned the heat down until it was bubbling gently.

"Now then," she said, "we must keep the

water topped up till it's thoroughly cooked, and we must NOT let it boil dry." She said this bit very loudly, as if poor Kitty was as deaf as a post. She wasn't deaf, but it was true that she sometimes forgot things.

"When we leave this kitchen, we must both take our pingers with us," continued Miss McGee. "Here's yours, Kitty." The "pingers" were things that made a noise when the food you were cooking was ready, or needed looking at. Kitty's was a smart white one with digital numbers that shone in the dark. It was called Big Time and it bleeped rather than pinged. She had bought it one day in Mr Moat's corner shop. He sold all kinds of useful items.

Sometimes they saw Debbie in the shop. Mr Moat was her mum's brother and he was Debbie's "Uncle Ted". When it was the holidays, Debbie sometimes helped him, putting things in bags and weighing things, but it was so long since the old ladies had seen her, or her mum, they were beginning to wonder if they had left the town altogether and gone to live somewhere else.

Big Time was the latest thing in pingers. In her quiet way, Kitty could be quite trendy. Miss McGee's pinger was a wind-up red one and it was an old and trusted friend, like the feet bowl. It had timed many puddings.

The old ladies never stayed in the kitchen at boiling time because the process took ages and the room got much too hot and steamy. With their pingers in their pockets, they went off into their own parts of the house. Miss McGee's was set to ping in half an hour when she would go and top up the water in the pan. Kitty's was set to bleep half an hour later, when she would do the same. Turn and turn about, every half hour, they would make sure the precious pudding never boiled dry. Only Nicholas remained in the kitchen, curled up in his basket next to the cooker. He kept looking up at the boiling saucepan; he was better than any dog.

"He's guarding our pudding," said Miss McGee. "Good old Nicholas."

"Good, dear cat," whispered Kitty. "What would we do without you?"

Kitty had plenty of time to spare before Big Time bleeped so she went back to sit in her chair by the window and stared down into Golden Square. She was a patient sort of lady. She believed that if she stayed there long enough, something was bound to happen. It was just a question of waiting.

She had learned about waiting from Nicholas. He would sit for hours, patiently waiting for a mouse to creep out from under a table or chair, where it had gone to hide (19 Golden Square had quite a few mice). He knew that, if he waited long enough, the mouse would reappear in the end. He was a brilliant mouser. Miss McGee said that Nicholas's paw control was the best she had ever come across, and she knew about cats because she'd been brought up on a farm. Kitty, who was a town person, had only ever known one cat, Nicholas, but she loved him with all her heart.

So did Miss McGee, but she never said it aloud, neither of them did, though each knew what the other was feeling. In this way, although very different from each other, the two old ladies were exactly the same.

Now perhaps Kitty had nodded off in her chair, or perhaps she had been looking away at the moment the person appeared on the scene. She couldn't remember afterwards. But what was for certain was this: on the afternoon of the pudding boiling a real child appeared down in the garden, in the middle of Golden Square.

It was a boy and he was very small, about three years old perhaps. He had a red something on his top half, and a blue something on his bottom half, and a floppy yellow something on his head. From her upstairs window Kitty

28

couldn't see what any of these things were.

The minute she saw him, she stood up and made her way downstairs to the front door. From the hook where it had hung for years and years she took the large, heavy key which unlocked the gate into the gardens. She only had one pocket in her skirt and it was quite little so, to make room for the key, which she absolutely must NOT lose, she removed Big Time and put it on the hall table. After all, she would only be out of the house for a very few minutes.

Chapter Four

The spiky, black gate which let people into the garden was not only shut, it was locked. This meant that the little boy must have climbed over the spikes *or* that he had been lifted inside, and left there. Kitty did not approve of either of these things: the iron spikes were dangerous and the garden was lonely and the boy was very small indeed. She could see him clearly now; he was wearing a bright red jersey and tiny, bright blue jeans and a floppy woollen hat the colour of a daffodil. Underneath, his hair was a great mass of golden curls; it looked as if he'd not yet had his first grown-up haircut.

Kitty unlocked the gate and went into the garden. She shut it behind her carefully, locked it again and walked up the path towards the child. "My name's Kitty," she told him. "I live at Number 19 with my friend Miss McGee and we have a cat called Nicholas. Do you have a pet?"

The small boy looked at her uncertainly. He had enormous, glossy brown eyes and a small, sweet mouth, all folded like the petals of a flower, but his lips were quivering. Kitty turned away, pretending she had lost all interest because she knew all about that particular look; it meant that he was about to cry.

Ignoring him, she started to poke about under the leafless shrubs on the edge of the little pond. "You find lovely things here," she said, as if to herself (but just loud enough for the little boy to hear, which of course was the whole idea). "Look... here's a lovely leaf that's slowly turning into a skeleton... and here's a perfectly round pebble... and here's... here's a frog! My goodness me..." The little boy was following her now and every time she bent down to look at something he bent down too. Round and round the garden they went, peacefully collecting things.

This game went on for quite a while but then it was as if the little boy suddenly remembered something quite different, or had decided to play his own game. He started to make a very particular kind of noise. "Chu... chu... chu..." and as he did so he lifted up the dry, twiggy branches of the shrubs, to peer underneath them. "Chu... chu... chu..." he kept calling.

"Is that a train game?" asked Kitty. "Can I play too? Chu... chu... chu..." she went, up and down the paths and round the pond. "We're great big steam trains," she told him, "we're not silly diesels... chu... chu... chu..." But at this the little boy slowed down, shook his head very solemnly and began to chew his fingers. Then he let out the most enormous HOWL.

It was quiet in Golden Square, and already quite dark. There were no doctors or dentists around in any case, because it was Saturday. In the silence, the cry of the little boy felt as big as an earthquake, and Kitty panicked. "Please don't cry, dear," she said, going up to him. "Please don't cry—" and then something suddenly burst out of the bushes, something resembling a big, red, flapping monster.

"Timothy!" it bellowed. "Timothy Joe! Come here this minute! We are terribly late. Your daddy's been sitting in the car for a whole ten minutes and he's extremely cross."

Kitty took a few steps backwards. She didn't like loud noises, or people that shouted. In this respect she was like Nicholas. But the red monster (who turned out to be a rather tall lady in a raincoat the colour of holly berries, with a red hat to match and curly fair hair), came right up to her. "What are *you* doing here?" she said, quite rudely.

"I... I live here," Kitty whispered, her insides turning into wobbly snakes, as they tended to do when she was nervous. "I live at Number 19, with my friend Miss McGee. We are your neighbours. I was so pleased to see your little boy in the garden that I came down to say hello. It's lovely to have a family in the square again. We so miss Debbie and her mum, you see. They've gone to live in the Town Flats, to escape the damp. Debbie was like a granddaughter to us."

For a second the very red lady looked slightly less ferocious, but then somebody nearby sounded a car horn three times. The driver was getting impatient. Without a word she swept the small boy off his feet and stuffed him under her arm like a large parcel. "I'm sorry but we really are horribly LATE," she said, moving off towards the gate.

Kitty ran ahead of her and unlocked it, but the lady did not say thank you, not even when Kitty called out, "I'll see to the gate – let us know if we can be of any help to you," because she really did want to be a good neighbour.

She watched the woman strap Timothy Joe into a car seat and climb into the car herself, next to a worried-looking man with spectacles who was the driver. She watched the car move away from the pavement and disappear from the square. Then she went back into the garden and sat for a while by the little pond, thinking about how angry the mother had been, how roughly she'd stuffed the little boy under her arm and how she'd not said thank you for anything.

Perhaps she wasn't his mother. Perhaps she was his nanny, or an "au pair" person, or even an aunt. Perhaps she was cross because she thought he'd got lost. But Kitty had been in the garden too, they had both been there, with the gate locked. She couldn't understand it at all. Next time she saw Debbie's mum in the square she would ask her if she knew anything about this fierce lady. Mrs Springer got to hear all sorts of gossip as she did her cleaning jobs.

Kitty sat for ages by the pond, turning the mystery over in her mind, then started to walk home very slowly, swishing the fallen leaves about with her flat, brown shoes. Little children liked swishing through leaves, especially when they were nice and crunchy, but these particular leaves had turned soggy. They had been on the pavement rather too long; it was too near Christmas for good crispy leaves.

Christmas! Kitty suddenly remembered the pudding, and Big Time, ticking away on the hall table in Number 19. Even though she was quite an old lady, she was still quite fit and so, picking up the hem of her long coat so as not to trip, she *ran* all the way home.

Chapter Five

As she puffed up the steps to the front door it opened all by itself, as if by magic. But Miss McGee was standing just behind it, her face all swollen with red rage, and there was a sickening smell and a haze in the air, as if the house had recently been on fire.

"I'm sorry, McGee," Kitty whimpered, knowing that her friend was about to explode about the pudding. "But I got held up in the garden. There really *is* a family with children at Number 26, well, there's a child, a dear little boy called Timothy Joe. It's wonderful."

But Miss McGee took no notice. "You went out, Kitty," she said, through gritted teeth, "and you left your timer behind you, and you forgot. My pudding's boiled dry, my beautiful pudding that cost me all that time and effort and money. There's a horrible mess all over the kitchen. It's a tragedy."

Kitty didn't answer, there was no point. She had seen Miss McGee in this angry mood before. What she must do was to put matters right as quickly as possible. She walked past her friend and went down the basement stairs into the kitchen, to see what she could do.

The haze down below was worse than in the hall: it was like thick fog and the horrible burnt smell made Kitty cough. She pulled out a hanky, squashed it against her nose, and spluttered into it. Her eyes began to stream but she could see, though everything was rather blurred, McGee's very best saucepan, all blackened with soot, and the pudding basin cracked right in half and, on the ceiling, a huge, dark ring, like a thundercloud.

"It's a tragedy," McGee repeated. "It's a real tragedy." Sagging down on to the nearest chair, she began to cry.

One part of Kitty was very sorry indeed but another part wasn't. Yes, it was terrible that she had forgotten the pudding but it wasn't the end of the world. She pointed this out to Miss McGee. "I'm really sorry, McGee," she told her, "but I was so excited about the new family. Listen, I'll paint the ceiling this afternoon; I'll stand on the table and I'll paint it, and I'll buy you a new pan for Christmas. It'll be an extra present. And I'll make another pudding for us, I'll do it right now." Picking up a cookery book, she started to turn the pages, she even started to hum.

It was the humming that did it, the humming

was the last straw to her friend McGee. "I don't want you to make another pudding," she wailed. "It's a tragedy."

It was Kitty's turn to get cross now. "Don't be silly, Florence," she snapped. "If you call spoiling a silly old pudding a tragedy, what do you call it if something really awful happens? What do you call it if someone has a terrible accident, or even dies? Now that's what *I* call a tragedy."

McGee did not reply. Instead she snatched up the lid of the saucepan, which was lying on the kitchen floor, and hurled it at Kitty's head. She missed and the lid hit a row of plates on a dresser and broke two of them. McGee, who had been sniffing miserably, now started to howl in earnest. In complete silence, like a person on television with the sound switched off, Kitty raised the cookery book she had been reading to find the pudding recipe, and threw it across the room in her friend's direction. She missed, too, (neither of the old ladies was a very good shot), and the book plopped into the sink where the pages spread out like wings. "Now my best cookery book's ruined as well!" McGee wailed, and she buried her face in her hands.

"You are RIDICULOUS!" screeched Kitty.

"Not so ridiculous as YOU," screeched Miss McGee.

Then she threw a wooden spoon at Kitty, then a nutmeg grater, and Kitty threw another cookery book and an egg, and they both screeched and screeched.

In the middle of it all, Nicholas, who had come running in through his cat-flap for tea, ran out again, and pelted right along all four sides of Golden Square and away, and was gone all that night.

And in the morning, when the two rather shamefaced old ladies met in the kitchen for their breakfast, he was still missing.

Chapter Six

They didn't notice at first, they were too busy being embarrassed, creeping around the kitchen and making their separate breakfasts. Normally they helped one another and shared things.

"Excuse *me*," grunted Miss McGee, "but I need to get the sugar basin down from that shelf," and "Excuse *me*," muttered Kitty, "I need to get myself some butter from the fridge." But in reaching for this and that, they bumped into each other. Miss McGee burst out laughing and patted Kitty's shoulder and Kitty squeezed Miss McGee's arm (though they were not huggy people) and they both said, "Aren't we *silly*?" and the quarrel was over. They had known each other for so long, you see, and they were such good friends. Having arguments was a waste of time.

Soon they were sitting at the kitchen table making a list. Christmas was coming and everybody made lists at Christmas; there was so much to do and to buy, even when you lived very quiet lives like Kitty and Miss McGee. The first thing was to get another pudding and they decided to buy one from Mr Moat at the corner shop. He sold excellent puddings, "as good as homemade", or so he told his customers.

Kitty said she would pay because she'd burned theirs, but Miss McGee said no, because that wasn't right, and that they would both pay. A tiny new quarrel was just starting up when

Kitty suddenly interrupted herself and said, "McGee, it's extremely quiet. Where is Nicholas?"

Miss McGee stared down at her feet. "I don't know, I've not seen him this morning. Didn't he come in when you boiled the kettle, for your first-thing cup of tea?" (Kitty always woke early and took a cup back to bed with her, till it got light.)

"No," Kitty said. "I thought he might be with you." (Nicholas adored the fat pillows on Miss McGee's bed and sometimes snuggled right underneath them, especially during cold weather.) "I've not seen Nicholas since—" then she stopped because the rest of the sentence was going to have been "—since I threw the saucepan lid and the wooden spoon and the nutmeg grater and we shouted." She didn't say any of this because it was too embarrassing.

Nicholas didn't come in for his breakfast and the rest of the morning was spent looking for him. They looked in their bedrooms and they looked in their sitting rooms and they looked in their spare rooms. Kitty climbed up to the dark, cobwebby attic on her long legs and searched among all the empty boxes and spare rolls of this and that which might come in useful one day. She unfolded all the spare paper shopping bags which they had hoarded away, and shook them out because Nicholas liked hiding in bags. It had occurred to her that he might have decided to hibernate this winter, like hedgehogs and tortoises. The weather was very cold and going to sleep until it warmed up again was such a good idea. But she couldn't find Nicholas.

Meanwhile, Miss McGee was searching in the cellar which ran all the way under the house. She didn't much like it down there; it was clammy and cold and there were lots of spiders. She only went into the cellar to get her jam jars when it was time for making jellies and jams and marmalade. Nicholas liked warm, snug places.

He would only be down in the cellar if someone had shut him in by accident. But nobody had.

"Nicholas!" dumpy Miss McGee called into the echoey darkness and "Nicholas!" echoed the chilly damp walls in a kind of mockery.

"Nicholas!" shouted skinny Kitty who had climbed daringly on to the roof, through the attic skylight (after all, most cats loved climbing). "Nicholas!" mimicked the red roof tiles, spitefully. Upon Golden Square and the streets all round, an unearthly quiet had fallen. Kitty closed up the skylight and went downstairs to find Miss McGee. In her heart she knew that Nicholas was nowhere in the house. He had run away, because of their noisy quarrel.

All this looking had made the two old ladies very tired so, after their lunch, they dozed in their chairs. But when the church clock in the square bonged loudly, four times, they didn't put the kettle on for tea, which was their usual habit, they wrapped up warmly and went walking in

46

the cold December air. Miss McGee went towards one end of the little town and Kitty went towards the other.

Up and down the wintry streets they plodded, calling and calling for their little lost cat. They called "Nicholas" high and they called it low. Miss McGee used her silky-soft voice, the kind she used when she was spoiling Nicholas and had a special treat for him, and Kitty used her silly, high-pitched voice which always brought him running in from the garden because it meant *food*. But no cat came bounding along in response to either of these voices, and no one at all had seen him. They stopped every person they met and asked.

Then, when it was almost dark, and they were walking disconsolately to meet each other from opposite ends of Golden Square, they saw what looked very like a fluffy little cat, all gingery pale and making a rolling, haphazard progress along the pavement towards them.

"Nicholas!" exclaimed Kitty with joy and she bent down to stroke him. But because of the rain and the mist, she wasn't wearing her spectacles, and what rubbed up against her legs wasn't a nice, warm, furry thing at all, it was a big, wet, torn, brown paper bag that the wind had blown along the pavement. "Ugh!" she cried, and kicked it away. Normally she would have scrunched it up very small and taken it to the nearest litter bin, but she didn't. Instead, she pretended she had something in her eye and she turned away from Miss McGee who had been scurrying up, all hopeful. She wanted to hide her tears.

"Now come on, Kitty," Miss McGee said sensibly when she saw the bag, and she tucked her arm into her friend's. "It's no good crying over spilt milk."

This is nothing to do with spilt milk, Kitty said to herself, while allowing Miss McGee to propel her along the pavements of Golden Square. *It's to do with a burnt pudding and throwing pan lids and shouting and a lost cat.* But she didn't say any of this out loud because Miss McGee was being so kind and, after all, it was Kitty who had burned the pudding and made the quarrel. So instead she said what, in her heart, she did not actually believe, which was, "He'll come back, McGee, when he's forgiven us."

"Oh, I'm sure he will," murmured Miss McGee, not believing it either, because Nicholas always came in very promptly for his meals, he was a greedy little cat. Something must have happened to him, something was wrong.

As they passed Number 26, the front door suddenly opened and the tall lady with the curly fair hair, the one whom Kitty had taken to be an angry, all-in-red monster, came out and peered down the street. She held Timothy Joe in her arms and he was wearing white pyjamas with blue dots on. In a lighted window, they could see the head of a great, black rocking horse.

Kitty tried to slow Miss McGee down. "Hello," she called out in a friendly voice. "Horrid old evening, isn't it?" And she was just going to ask the lady if she'd seen a cat resembling Nicholas when, having looked quickly down the street again, to left and to right, the red lady went inside and shut the door with a loud slam.

"Charming!" said Miss McGee, quickening her pace so that Kitty was almost sliding after her along the pavement. "If that's the kind of neighbour she is, then I don't want neighbours, thank you very much."

But Kitty was thinking how very sad the lady's face had looked, and how sad it had looked in the garden, under the crossness. "I think they might have some sorrow, McGee," she whispered. But her friend didn't hear, she was too busy trying to find her door key in one of her many pockets. She believed you could never have too many pockets in your clothes, a view with which Kitty didn't always agree, though if she had had two pockets in her skirt the day before, she would have been able to put Big Time into one of them and taken it with her into Golden Square. Then the pudding wouldn't have burned. Then Nicholas wouldn't have run away.

When they got inside, Kitty and Miss McGee went straight downstairs to the kitchen to see if he had come back in their absence. But he hadn't. All was exactly as they had left it. His special cushion, in its basket by the cooker, was still plumped up and undented. His bowl of deluxe crunchy food (left out to lure him home) was uneaten and his basin of water was undrunk. His three favourite toys, a white ping-pong ball, a patchwork mouse and a fluffy black spider with only three legs, were exactly where Kitty had placed them. It all felt very catless indeed.

Miss McGee got busy, tied on her apron and made them both scrambled eggs on toast. The eggs, supplied by Mr Moat, Debbie's Uncle Ted who ran the corner shop, were as yellow as buttercups and beautifully fresh. The bread for the toast had been made by Miss McGee herself and that too was delicious. On top she sprinkled some fresh green parsley chopped very small. Kitty had cleverly grown this in a plant pot and it was still alive, in spite of the winter's cold. The meal looked and smelt yummy, but after a few mouthfuls Kitty put down her knife and fork.

"I'm sorry, McGee," she said. "But I have no appetite. I keep thinking about Nicholas."

"So do I," her friend replied, and she too pushed her plate away. "It's awful. Where can the poor little thing have got to?"

They threw their uneaten teas away and washed up in total silence. Both had their ears pricked up to catch the tiniest mewing, purring or scratching sound, but a great silence hung over 19 Golden Square. Very much earlier than usual, they said goodnight to one another and crept away to bed.

Up in their rooms they both said their prayers. Miss McGee couldn't kneel down any more because her stout little legs were much too stiff. To pray, she always sat in a special chair where she would arrange her hands neatly in her lap and close her eyes. That night she said a little prayer to St Anthony because he was the special saint for lost things. Very politely, she asked him to find Nicholas and to bring him home again.

Kitty's special saint was called St Jude, a saint who looked after hopeless causes and hopeless people. Miss McGee had said *she* was "hopeless" when she offered to make a new Christmas pudding, but this wasn't the reason she chose St Jude. She chose him because she was afraid. She wasn't going to admit this to her friend but she was afraid in case Nicholas had already been killed on the huge new motorway that roared all day and all night just a few miles beyond the town, a noise they could hear quite clearly in Golden Square, when the wind blew the sound towards them. Lots of animals had been run over on that awful road and she feared one of them might be Nicholas.

"Please, dear St Jude," she said, kneeling up very straight at the side of her bed, "don't let such an awful thing have happened to our dear little cat," and before rising from her knees she added, "and please look after the children in Number 26, and their mummy and daddy." She put this bit in as well because her "bones", which sometimes told her things in a mysterious way she could not explain to anybody, were telling her quite clearly that the new family was in some kind of trouble, something much worse than the vanishing of Nicholas.

She had said "children" in the prayer because, even though she'd seen only Timothy Joe, there had definitely been *two* bicycles, on moving-in day.

Chapter Seven

Next morning there was still no Nicholas so, immediately after breakfast, Kitty and Miss McGee sat down once again at their kitchen table and began to make a list. But this list was nothing whatever to do with Christmas, which was getting very near now. It was about their missing cat.

"We must have a plan of action," said Miss McGee.

"I agree, we must have a *campaign*," added Kitty. Her father had been a soldier, and had won medals for being brave, so she knew all about "campaigns".

"First we must make a list of really useful people," said Miss McGee. "Take these names down, please, Kitty." So Kitty unscrewed her fountain pen and smoothed out a stout paper bag to write on. (The old ladies never threw anything away, not unless it fell to bits.) Kitty could do beautifully neat writing: she'd had lots of practice, when she taught the little children. Miss McGee called out names and she copied them down carefully. When the list was complete they both looked at it for a long time, and both had the same, rather depressing thought. It was very short indeed and had very few names on it.

Kitty gave a sad little cry. "We have no friends, McGee; we have grown so old, we have no friends left."

"Nonsense!" Miss McGee said briskly, inspecting

the list. "It's not our fault if people keep moving away. And we do have friends, Kitty, and what matters is the *kind* of people on our list. One really good friend is worth ten bad ones. Now come along, let's go through the names and make a plan."

Together they bent their white heads over the piece of paper. *Lily Lyon*, was the first name Kitty had written down. Lily was a traffic warden who patrolled Golden Square. She was dumpy and short with a fierce kind of face and lots of flyaway, iron-grey hair. Her job was to stick tickets on people's cars when they parked on the double yellow lines. The ticket meant the people had to pay money, for breaking the law. They were always getting mad with Lily, waving the tickets under her nose and shouting rude things. But Lily never shouted back. She would pretend she was deaf, or foreign, and didn't understand.

"Lily's a good person to help us," remarked

Miss McGee. "She knows what's going on round here; she's forever walking up and down."

"And she loves Nicholas," Kitty reminded her. "She always saves him a nice tasty bit out of her sandwich." (Nicholas loved cheese, and chicken, and bacon, and Lily's sandwiches were usually one of these three kinds.)

Next on the list was Mr Moat from the corner shop. "We must certainly tell him," said Miss McGee. "All the people with cats come to him to buy his special pets' mince. We could ask him to put a notice up in his shop, a "missing cat" notice, and if, by chance, Debbie's there, or her mum, we could ask them to help us too."

But Kitty looked doubtful about this. "Mrs Springer won't be doing any cleaning over the Christmas break," she said "And anyhow, Debbie's not been to see us for ages. I do keep wondering, McGee, if they've moved house. If only they had a telephone at the Flats, I would ring them and tell them about Nicholas going missing." She rather thought that Mrs Springer couldn't afford to have a phone put in at her new place and she couldn't afford one of those mobiles either. She probably used the public call box, just outside the tall, draughty building round which the wind sometimes blew, frightening the two old ladies at the very thought.

Mr Pick, the dentist, who had a surgery on the corner of the square, was another name on the list. Every lunch hour he changed into some shiny blue shorts and puffed round and round Golden Square about a hundred times. It made the old ladies feel weary just looking at him, but he always waved to them, however fast he was running.

"We must tell Mr Pick," said Miss McGee. "He can ask all his patients to keep a lookout for Nicholas, and perhaps he'll print out some "missing cat" notices for us. He's just got a wonderful new colour printer machine, he told me all about it."

Now they were actually doing something,

Miss McGee felt much more cheerful. But Kitty didn't. Inside she was sagging, like a burst balloon. She just couldn't get rid of her hopeless "St Jude" feeling about poor lost Nicholas.

"Reg," she said, consulting the list. "Reg, from A1 Cabs, we could get him to help us." Kitty and Miss McGee didn't own a car and they didn't go anywhere much. But when they had to go on a special journey, they would ring up Reg and ask him to take them in his red taxi.

Kitty was hatching a rather sad little plan of her own. It was to get Reg to drive her very slowly along that awful motorway, to see if poor Nicholas was lying dead by the side of the road. If he had been run over, then she wanted to know as soon as possible. She would take him home and put him in a box and bury him in their tiny back garden.

She said nothing about this plan to Miss McGee, who was now quite cheerful, adding more names to the list and making her own copy, so that not a minute should be wasted. Each of them was to do different things in the campaign. Wherever they were in the town, they must, of course, call out Nicholas's name. Kitty would visit the people on one half of the list and Miss McGee would do the other half and they would meet at lunch time and compare notes.

One thing about the list made Kitty really sad, and it was this: apart from Debbie Springer, who had almost certainly left the town by now, there were no children on it, and she knew that children had bags of energy. When she'd worked in her school she would sometimes watch the boys and girls tearing around the playground, laughing and shouting, and she would think to herself, *A handful of children like that could change the entire world.*

When Miss McGee wasn't looking, she wrote something extra at the bottom of her list: "Number 26, Golden Square", because she had another plan. She would go and ask if there were any other children living there, bigger children than Timothy Joe, who might help them look for Nicholas.

After breakfast the old ladies set off on their campaign. Miss McGee soon found Lily Lyon. She was outside Number 11 where a doctor had rooms, listening to a screaming young man who was sitting astride a pizza delivery bike. "Five minutes," he was yelling. "I was only away for five minutes and I get this SILLY TICKET! Why don't you go and chase some REAL criminals?"

Lily said mildly, "I'm very sorry, I'm only doing my job," which was what she always said, when she wasn't pretending to be deaf, or foreign.

"Shame," said Miss McGee, catching up with Lily, who had walked away from the angry young man. "And what a funny time to be delivering pizza, at ten o'clock in the morning."

But Lily didn't agree. "You see all kinds of things, doing my job," she answered. "For example, that house over there gets pizzas and stuff delivered at very odd hours. Perhaps the people living there work nights in factories. Perhaps they're too tired to cook when they get home."

"Which house?"

"Number 26."

"Oh, the one that's just been sold?" said Miss McGee. "How very curious. There's a young couple living in that house, a couple with a toddler... Anyway, why I've come, Lily, is because we've lost Nicholas; he vanished, the day before yesterday." (She didn't mention the quarrel or the throwing things across the kitchen or the shouting.)

Lily's mouth puckered. "Oh *no*! I love your Nicholas and I was hoping to see him today. I've got bacon sandwiches."

"Well, we're not panicking," said Miss McGee (though this wasn't quite true: she was panicking, but not quite so much as Kitty). "Please will you keep your eyes open, and let us know if you see him?"

"Of course I will," answered Lily. "You can rely on me. Have you thought of saying that there's a reward? You know, fifty pounds for the person who brings him back safe and sound. That would be a useful sum of money at Christmas time."

Miss McGee hesitated. Fifty pounds was a lot to her and Kitty. They only had their old age pensions to pay their bills.

"The thing is," said Lily, "he may have been stolen. A pretty cat like Nicholas would be a very nice Christmas present for somebody."

Miss McGee gripped her arm. "Lily," she said, "don't even *think* about such a thing. Kitty's in quite a bad way about this, she's fretting." She was in quite a bad way herself, but she was determined not to show it. One of them had to be strong.

A gigantic woman in a glossy green raincoat, and with amazing black, corkscrew hair, was striding angrily towards them waving a parking ticket. Lily turned away. "I think I'll be foreign this morning," she whispered in Miss McGee's ear. "Good luck, in your search for Nicholas. I'm sure he'll turn up."

"Hope so," the old lady answered, setting off in the direction of the corner shop.

It was depressing talking to Mr Moat. "Fur hats," he said solemnly. "People steal cats in the winter time to make fur hats."

Miss McGee grabbed his hand. "Don't even think of such a thing, Mr Moat," she told him. "And if Kitty comes in to see you, don't mention it to her. Promise?"

"I promise, Miss McGee," said the shopkeeper solemnly. "Now write out your missing cat notice and I'll stick it in my window. I expect the little blighter will turn up." But he didn't sound at all convinced.

Then Miss McGee said, "Is Debbie still around, Mr Moat? I've not see her or her mum for ages."

The shopkeeper shook his head. "I've not either. I think it's the cleaning jobs in the square: they've dried up. The people in the offices all got together and decided to use a big firm instead, *Dusters* it's called. They said it works out cheaper, or something, so they got rid of our Sylvia. So she's working on the other side of town now. Shame, isn't it? I miss my little Debbie, she's a good little worker. So's her mum."

"The thing is," Miss McGee said slowly, "we could get Debbie to help us to look for Nicholas. She's so fond of him, and patient, though I'm afraid he tends to prefer old ladies to children! I suppose one of us could take a walk to the Flats to ask, though we don't fancy going up to the top in that lift."

"No need to," Mr Moat explained. "Our Sylvia's got a mobile now, for the cleaning jobs. She says she has to be "on call", in case someone wants her in a hurry. Here's the number," and he wrote it down for her on a brown paper bag.

Miss McGee folded it up carefully and put it in her handbag. When she got home she would copy the number into her address book and save the paper bag. It didn't do to waste things.

After this, she set off for home, though she took a long way round and walked down Grendel Lane, past the deserted schoolhouse where Kitty had once been a teacher. It was sad, looking at the empty buildings which used to be noisy with the chattering of children. The school had closed down three years ago and its few remaining children had been sent to another school. Miss McGee called across the empty playground, but her voice held no conviction. "Nicholas! Nicholas!" But nothing stirred except a little scurry of dead leaves round the feet of the rusty climbing frame.

Across the yard were two stone archways labelled "BOYS" and "GIRLS". Out from under GIRLS wandered Kitty. She looked sheepish when she saw her friend. "I was just poking about," she said. "I thought he might have squeezed into the school and not been able to get out again. There are gaps now, under some of the doors."

Miss McGee shivered. "Rats," she said. "That will be rats, gnawing at the wood. It'll be a good thing when they pull this place down, if you ask me." But Kitty looked sad. The schoolhouse was full of very happy memories for her.

"Come on," Miss McGee continued. "He's not here; we've both called him and he would have come, or at least we'd have heard him mewing. I do have a bit of good news, Debbie's mum's got a mobile phone and Mr Moat's given me the number. She's working on the other side of town now but they still live in the Flats. So we could get Debbie to help us, Kitty, we could ring when we get home."

Kitty brightened up at this news of Debbie and set off along Grendel Lane with a lighter step. But when they came to a tall garden gate with 26 painted on it, she stopped. "This must be the garden belonging to the new people, the people in the Square," she murmured, and she peeped through a knot-hole in the wood. "They've got a climbing frame, too!" she told Miss McGee excitedly. "That proves it, there *are* children."

"Only one, only that toddler," muttered Miss McGee. "You're getting obsessed by that family, Kitty. They don't want to be friendly and that's that. Come on, let's go home for our elevenses. Nicholas may well be back by now."

But he wasn't. The ping-pong ball and the spider and the mouse, the undented cushion and the food and the water were all exactly as they had left them. And now they were both thinking something that they dared not say in words to each other, and it was this: the longer his absence grew, and the more the time passed, the less and less likely it was that Nicholas would ever come home again.

For example, if he'd got lost then he must by now be quite hopelessly lost. And if he'd been injured on that horrible motorway, and nobody had come to his aid, then by now he most definitely would have died. To cheer themselves up they rang Debbie's mum on her mobile to ask for help in the search, but nobody answered. The telephone rang and rang into an empty silence but no voice at the other end said, "This is Mrs Springer, please leave a message." or anything like that. There was just the ringing, going on and on, which made their sad feelings even sadder and somehow made them feel even more helpless.

They sat side by side at the kitchen table, drank their coffee and nibbled half-heartedly at Miss McGee's special chewy treacle biscuits and didn't say a single word to each other. But, though it was all extremely silent, the air was thick and humming with their private, terrible thoughts.

Chapter Eight

That afternoon, while Miss McGee was having a nap, Kitty slipped out. First she called at Mr Pick's, the dentist's, with a photo of Nicholas. He had promised to make some notices for them with his new colour printer and the photo was to be part of it. It could be nailed on to trees and put through people's letter boxes.

Mr Plackett, the postman, the friend whom

they'd forgotten, at first, to put on their list of helpers (and how *could* they have forgotten? He was Nicholas's greatest fan and had said that he would like to have used his tail as a feather duster) told them that, unfortunately, he was not allowed to post people's private notices through letter boxes, it was against the rules. But he promised he would tell everybody he saw to keep a sharp lookout for the prettiest and cleverest and friendliest ginger cat they had ever seen, a cat who'd disappeared from Kitty and Miss McGee's.

Kitty made excuses and hurried away while Mr Plackett was still talking. All these praises brought the catness of Nicholas, who was now hopelessly lost, so close to her, and made him so real, that she could hardly bear it.

After visiting the dentist's she went to the post office, to collect her old-age pension. She wrapped the bank notes round the coins and thrust them deep into the pocket of her long winter coat. Kitty didn't take a handbag out shopping because she was always losing things. She began to make her way towards the taxi rank which was several streets away, in the new shopping precinct, where Reg would be waiting for her in his glossy red cab.

On her way there she had to pass Mr Moat's corner shop and whom should she see, weighing oranges out into a paper bag, but Debbie! She had grown a bit taller and a bit thinner since they had last seen each other, and she didn't have thick plaits any more; her hair, which was red like her mother's, had been cut and now waved round her face in the same kind of curls.

"Debbie!" shouted Kitty. "Is it really you?"

Debbie, whipping round and smiling, her teeth gleaming white in her round freckled face, shouted, "Kitty! Yes, it really is!"

They had a little hug, right there on the pavement, and Debbie said, "Thanks a lot for the money," because Kitty and Miss McGee had sent her some for Christmas, so she could choose a present for herself. Old ladies didn't really know what modern girls like Debbie wanted any more. Then Kitty explained about Nicholas being lost and how she was about to take a taxi and go slowly along the motorway, "just in case".

At once Debbie squared her shoulders. "Right," she said, in a very firm voice. "I'm going to ask Uncle Ted if I can come with you. Wait there a sec."

Almost at once, she was back. "He says I can come. I'm staying at the shop while Mum's visiting Gran in Blackpool; she's taken her a Christmas present but Gran's laid up with a cold and she doesn't want me to catch it."

Debbie's gran was her dad's mother. Mr Springer had died a long time ago, in an accident, in the factory where he worked. But Debbie still remembered him: she had shown the old ladies a photo. Mrs Springer was not the sort of person to mope around and feel sorry for herself, she just got on with things, and so did Debbie. They were two brave people.

Kitty explained to Reg that they wanted to ride up and down the new motorway; they wanted to be driven very slowly in both directions, so that they could look for their missing cat along the verges. She talked in a very low voice and she did not explain all this to Debbie. She was rather vague, and spoke as if Nicholas was almost certainly still alive but merely lost, that he might be stuck in a field on the edge of the motorway, having lost his bearings and needing to be rescued.

Secretly she knew perfectly well that, if she did find Nicholas, he was almost certain to be dead, hit by a car or lorry. It was possible that his poor little body would be very badly injured, perhaps even squashed flat. But Kitty, like Debbie and her mum, was a brave person, her father having been a soldier who had won medals, and his great bravery had been passed on to her. She had his fighter's blood. She had brought her gardening gloves with her, and a thick plastic bag, and if she found the body of

Nicholas she would pull her gloves on, close her eyes, scoop it into the bag and take him home. Of course she did not mention any of this to Debbie and all this equipment was hidden deep in the big, useful pocket of her winter coat, underneath her pension money.

Reg, the cab driver, had known Kitty and Miss McGee for a very long time and he was their friend, as well as their taxi man. He wasn't a cat person, he loved dogs, but he was very sorry about Nicholas. "Don't you worry, Miss Kitty," he said, as she and Debbie climbed into his taxi. "I'm sure he'll turn up, we'll not find him on the motorway, you mark my words." But he agreed to do what she had requested and they set off steadily for the great, screaming road.

It was horrible on the motorway. Even the cars in the slow lane seemed to be going a hundred times faster than Reg, and all the drivers kept hooting and shaking their fists. But Reg was wonderful. He took no notice of them at all and just drove on quietly, going very slowly so that they could look carefully at anything lying by the side of the road on the hard shoulder. Three times Kitty asked him to stop, even though you weren't supposed to, and a policeman might have come to tell them off. But she decided she had to take this risk and that a policeman would understand. She would explain that Nicholas had got lost and how much she and Miss McGee were missing him and how Debbie had come along to help.

The first time Reg stopped it was so that they could look at a gingery object that turned out to be a fox. It looked quite perfect and not at all dead, just fast asleep.

"Ah," Debbie said. "That's a shame. But, did you know, Granny Kitty, they're always climbing into dustbins, to get at people's thrown-away food. They're getting to be a terrible nuisance. They make a real mess of people's gardens."

Debbie was a very practical sort of person

and Kitty had a strong feeling that, if they did find Nicholas, and if he were dead, Debbie would take charge and arrange things. She was so glad she had found her at Mr Moat's shop, and so glad she was helping in the search.

The second thing they found was a badger with a great, striped head. "Rare those are, Miss Kitty," Reg remarked. "Leastways, I've never seen one before, not a real 'un, only seen 'em in books."

"I've seen one before," Debbie told him, "and that one was dead too. We were in the country, near Uncle Ted's cottage. I think a car had hit it." Again, she didn't sound at all upset. It was what often happened to animals on busy roads, and that was that. At least, this is what Kitty decided Debbie must be thinking.

The third thing filled her with terror because it was a cat and not only that, it was a ginger one. But it wasn't Nicholas. This cat was much bigger, with white rings on its tail, which

Nicholas didn't have. Like the fox, it looked as if it was merely sleeping, but when Kitty looked at it properly and actually got out of the taxi for a minute to touch it, she found it was all stiff and cold. It had a collar on with a label attached and on this label was a phone number. Reg lent her a pen and Kitty wrote it down on the palm of her hand. The other side of the label said OSCAR.

Debbie seemed much sadder about this dead animal than she had been about the fox and the badger. "It's somebody's pet, Granny Kitty," she whispered, "or it wouldn't have a collar on, would it, or its phone number? Somebody must have loved it," she added. Then she said, "We had a cat like that once, but it got run over and I was so upset Mum said we'd better not have another one. And now we can't anyway. You're not allowed pets in the Flats."

When they had finished looking at poor Oscar Kitty called out, "Reg, you can go fast now; we're not looking any more, we've had enough for one day."

"But I can help again tomorrow, can't I?" Debbie said anxiously. She so wanted to be the person who found Nicholas for the two old ladies.

"You certainly can," Kitty told her, "if there are jobs to be done. A family has just moved into Golden Square and I want to try and get them to help us too. There's a little boy and I think he may have brothers and sisters. You could make friends with them."

Debbie's eyes shone. "I'd love that," she said. "I never see anybody, much, at the Flats. We're all on top of each other and there's nowhere to play."

Reg speeded up and pelted off towards the town. In no time at all they were back at the taxi rank. But when Kitty dug into her pocket for her pension Reg said he wouldn't accept any money. "It's a pleasure, Kitty," he said. "Just let me know when the little feller turns up and I'll give him a piece of my mind, worrying you and Miss McGee like this."

So Kitty, having taken Debbie back to Mr Moat's shop, went slowly away, thinking that if Nicholas did come home they would give a little party, or at the very least make a cake or do something to thank Reg, the postman, the dentist, Mr Moat at the shop and all the people who were kindly helping them.

More and more, however, she felt that they would not see Nicholas again, because when Reg had said, "When the little feller turns up," he had spoken in a flat and unbelieving way as if, really, he thought their cat had gone for ever but didn't like to say so. And in her heart, this is what Kitty thought too, and she rather believed it was what Debbie thought also, though she hadn't said so. The Springers always looked on the bright side of things; in that way they were more like Miss McGee than they were like Kitty.

On her way home she stopped in Golden Square. The windows of Number 26 were all lit up and through a blind she could see the shape of the great black rocking horse and the shadow of a child riding it, held on firmly by a shadowy, grown-up hand. This meant that the new neighbours were in, there was no doubt about it.

Very boldly, Kitty climbed up the five stone steps to the front door and looked for a bell. There it was, a beautifully polished brass one over a printed label that said *MR AND MRS JAMES ATKINSON*.

She pressed the bell and waited. Nothing happened so she pressed again. This time the rocking horse stopped rocking, but the human shadows stayed exactly where they were. All she could hear was a muffled shouting from inside. Then the front door opened and a dumpy little lady was looking up at her. She was wearing an apron and there was a duster in her hand.

Kitty said, "Please may I speak to Mrs Atkinson or to Mr Atkinson. My name's Kitty. I live across the way at Number 19 and our cat's gone missing."

For a moment the dumpy lady said nothing. Her eyes were searching Kitty's face and reading her lips. She looked very perplexed and it became clear that she did not understand.

"May I speak to one of the Atkinsons?" Kitty repeated, very slowly and patiently.

Suddenly, the little lady shook her head quite fiercely. "No visitors, no thank you, visitors. Is not possible, today. I tell missis." She took the opportunity to shake her duster out over the steps with a flourish, then turned away and closed the door slowly muttering, "Sorry, very sorry. No visitor is possible."

Kitty went straight home. She was more and more certain that there was some kind of trouble behind the newly painted door of Number 26, Golden Square. The mother had been so angry, out in the square, and had rushed off without even saying thank you. And the cleaning lady had clearly been instructed to keep all visitors away. And yet, Timothy Joe was certainly there, riding his rocking horse – unless the shadow behind the blind had been another little child. It was a mystery.

Later that night, the two old ladies sat with their bedtime cups of cocoa in Kitty's sitting room, which looked out over Golden Square. They were comparing notes and Miss McGee was writing everything down on a smart clipboard which Mr Pick had given them. She was delighted that Debbie had started to help, in the search for their lost cat.

"Such a sensible little girl, that Debbie Springer," she muttered, underlining everything very neatly, as if that alone would help to make Nicholas come back. "And her mother is so sensible too. How silly of the people in the square not to want her to do their cleaning any more. I have heard that those *Dusters* people charge very high prices. It's a shame. She's such a treasure."

"They might change their minds," said Kitty, "and she might come back and live in the square again. That'd be nice."

"Not in a damp flat covered with mould," Miss McGee reminded her.

"No. But it would be nice if they *did* come back," persisted Kitty, who did not easily give up on things.

The "lost cat" notices, complete with the photograph of Nicholas, were now ready and the old ladies had fifty each to distribute round the town. Next morning, when they had more energy, they planned to post them through people's letter boxes, stick them on lampposts and nail them to fences and to the trunks of trees. Nobody in that neighbourhood would be in any doubt at all about what had happened.

The notices said that a small ginger cat called Nicholas with a long, fluffy coat and a beautiful, plume-like tail was missing. A reward of fifty pounds was offered to the person who brought him back safe and sound to Kitty and Miss McGee, of Number 19 Golden Square.

Kitty sat by the window plucking up all her

courage to tell Miss McGee about her trip with Debbie up and down the motorway in Reg's taxi. This needed courage because McGee was bound to say it was silly and an absolute waste of money, even though Reg had not accepted any payment in the end.

She decided not to say anything, but for a different reason, which made everything seem even more hopeless than before. It was because Miss McGee had suddenly said to her, "By the way, while you were out this afternoon I rang the Cat Rescue office. I rang the vet too and nobody's handed Nicholas in to either of them. The Cat Rescue people said that if he'd been run over they would know, because you have to report that kind of thing. So that's good news, isn't it?"

"Very good news," whispered Kitty, thinking of those poor, dead animals she'd seen by the side of the motorway. She'd already rung the owners of Oscar to tell them that, very unfortunately, their cat had been run over, and they'd said thank you and that they would go and collect him. So people didn't always report these sad things and Nicholas could easily be dead anyway. But she said none of this to Miss McGee, just as she had said none of it to Debbie. It was no good upsetting people unless you absolutely had to.

Very soon the old ladies wished each other good night and climbed up the stairs to bed. Kitty said a prayer to St Jude again, because everything felt really hopeless now. She said thank you for the fact that Debbie Springer had turned up, and was helping them, and she slipped in an extra prayer for the Atkinsons at Number 26. Her bones were convincing her more and more that they were in very bad trouble indeed.

Chapter Nine

Next day Kitty and Miss McGee got very tired. They spent ages posting their cat notices through people's doors. Debbie helped, but even though there were now three of them, and Debbie was young and fit and could jump about and do things quickly, it was very hard work.

Sometimes the ·letter boxes were stiff, or wouldn't open at all, or shut with a snap on their fingers, and sometimes there wasn't one. Sometimes a dog barked ferociously behind a door and probably chewed the notice up the minute it hit the mat. Sometimes a voice called out, "Not today, thank you." It was very likely that lots of people simply threw the notices away. As they trudged around the town, the two ladies got more and more depressed.

Debbie did her very best to cheer them up. "I spoke to my mum on the phone," she told them. "She's still at Gran's and Gran said that you mustn't give up hope. She says that cats sometimes go missing for weeks and weeks and WEEKS and then they turn up again and they're as right as ninepence."

"As right as what, dear?" enquired Kitty.

"As ninepence," repeated Debbie. "I'm not really sure what it means exactly."

Kitty was thoughtful. "I remember people saying it when I was young. I think it means 'as good as before'."

"That sounds right," the little girl nodded. "Anyway, the main message from Gran was not to give up hope. She knows lots about cats."

Miss McGee said firmly, noticing that Kitty had gone rather droopy and sad, "I'm sure your Gran is right, Debbie, we must just go on looking for Nicholas and hoping for the best."

It was now nearly Christmas and after she'd finished helping with the notices, Debbie had to go back to the corner shop. Her mother was coming home from Gran's that afternoon. The council men had put up a Christmas tree in the middle of Golden Square and people on long ladders were decorating it with coloured lights. Wherever they went they heard Christmas carols wafting out of shop doorways, and everybody was rushing about shopping. But the general excitement only served to make the loss of Nicholas sharper and sadder for them.

They didn't feel like joining in the carol singing, or wrapping up presents, or eating mince pies. They wanted to be by themselves, to face up to the fact that a very important member of their tiny household was missing. Nicholas had been important; he had been like the children or the grandchildren that they had never had. He had loved them both the same and he had not had favourites, as some people did, and he had always said "thank you" by his loud, generous purring whenever they played with him, or gave him his meals. There was a dark, raw hole now in the household at 19 Golden Square and it was Nicholas-shaped.

Christmas Eve came. All the leaflets had been posted or stuck up for everyone to read, but no one had phoned them. Mr Plackett had helped a lot, fixing their notices on trees and fences, and Debbie had been brilliant. Miss McGee had phoned the Cat Rescue office again, and the vet, and the police station, just in case someone had handed Nicholas in, alive or dead. She had said, "It's best to *know*, Kitty," but nobody had seen him, nobody at all. Debbie rang from the Flats when she got home with her mum, just in case Nicholas had turned up again, but they had to say no, he had not.

"Right then," announced Miss McGee, in her most business-like voice. "We must accept that our search is over and we must now draw a line." And to show exactly what she meant, she took a thick, felt-tipped pen and ruled a neat line under the list of "helpers".

"Please don't let's give up just yet, McGee," pleaded Kitty and her voice was trembling; she wasn't feeling brave any more.

"No, we really must, Kitty. Dear Nicholas had a lovely life. If he is dead then 'God rest his soul', as people say, and if he's alive and gone to another home, then let's hope his new owners are enjoying him."

"That's what you said when the burglars got in, and stole your silver teapot," Kitty reminded her.

"Did I really?"

"You did. You said, 'Well, I just hope whoever's stolen that lovely teapot of mine is enjoying it.' But Nicholas isn't a teapot, McGee, he's a living, breathing—" and she was just going to say "human being" when she broke off, because Nicholas, marvellous as he was, was only a cat after all.

Miss McGee could see that Kitty was trying hard not to cry. She stood up, patted her friend's hand, and went into the pantry. "Come on, we'll have a nice glass of sherry each and a mince pie and a chocolate, to cheer ourselves up. It's nearly Christmas."

So the sherry was poured into two glittering glasses, the mince pies warmed through in the oven and the box of chocolates that kind Mr Pick had given them, was unwrapped.

"Cheers," said Miss McGee, raising her glass.

"Cheers," replied Kitty, raising hers.

But secretly they both felt one hundred per

cent miserable. There was nothing "cheering" to be said.

Christmas Day was very quiet for the two old ladies and they had no visitors at all. Sometimes McGee's cousin Albert came for Christmas, up from the country, but that year he didn't because there was illness among the cows on his farm. Sometimes Kitty's niece Jane came, with her jolly husband Peter and their three little children. But she couldn't come either, it was the year they had to go to Peter's family, at the seaside.

"I'm sure Jane would have come if she possibly could have done, dear," Miss McGee said soothingly to Kitty. "The children adore Nicholas. But at Christmas it has to be 'turn and turn about' with families, you know that." And there was nobody else who might have visited them; the old ladies had lived so long they didn't have any other relatives left, apart from the sort that lived in far-off places like Australia and Singapore.

Kitty was secretly hoping that Debbie and her mum might call by, especially now, when they were feeling so sad about Nicholas. But they didn't, they had gone to spend the day with Uncle Ted, not in the flat behind his shop but in his country cottage with its view of the hills, his cottage where he went on his days off and for holidays.

Miss McGee knew this because Debbie's mum had phoned up while Kitty was out calling for Nicholas, late on Christmas Eve. She would keep going into Golden Square and calling and calling, and McGee so wanted her to stop, it was getting silly.

Mrs Springer had just wanted to know if there was any news of Nicholas, and promised that the minute Christmas was over she and Debbie would be "back in circulation". This meant that Debbie would be on hand to look for Nicholas again

"Our Debbie's brilliant at finding lost

things," her mother said proudly. "I'm forever losing things and she always finds them." But Miss McGee had to tell her that there was no news at all. She did not add what she now feared, that there wasn't going to be any news, and that Nicholas had vanished without trace and was lost for ever and ever.

On Christmas morning the old ladies went to church. The streets were very quiet and a wind had swept Golden Square quite bare of its last remaining leaves. Even a cunning little cat like Nicholas, who liked to hide, would have shown up against such bareness and would have been heard mewing in such deep quiet. They did see a cat, a big black and white one, sitting on a window ledge with a bright Christmas ribbon round its neck. The sight saddened them.

Kitty wanted to ring the doorbell at Number 26 and say "Happy Christmas" to the Atkinsons. The house was lit up and the window below the rocking horse one had a Christmas tree winking with lights, but Miss McGee hurried her past.

"No, Kitty," she said firmly. "They don't want to be neighbourly, you must accept that."

In church they said their prayers, Kitty to St Jude, who cared about hopeless causes and people, and McGee to St Anthony who brought back lost things, even though she had drawn that thick black line underneath the search for Nicholas. There were lots of families, and zillions of children all running around with their new toys. Nobody stopped them because it was Christmas. Suddenly, Kitty saw Timothy Joe in the arms of the man she had seen waiting in the car.

"Happy Christmas, Timothy Joe," she called excitedly across the cold, echoey church. Timothy Joe waved a blue teddy at her and shouted back "Happy Kippiss." Then the man smiled at her very kindly and actually looked as if he might walk across the church and speak to her. But then she saw him look at his watch and shrug, crinkle his lips in a worried way and hurry off.

Nothing else happened that day. The two friends went home and cooked two crispy pieces of duck for their Christmas dinner. They ate a little of Mr Moat's pudding and had a little glass of port each and some chocolates – because it was Christmas and they must celebrate, even though they felt sad about Nicholas. He had adored Christmas, especially playing with all the scrunched-up wrapping paper, and hiding in the boxes which slippers and things had come in.

The only person they spoke to all day, was Miss McGee's Auntie Maggie, who was nearly a hundred but still lived on the family farm out in the country, with Cousin Albert and his wife to look after her. After this phone call they went up to Kitty's sitting room, which overlooked Golden Square. They sank into their chairs on opposite sides of the fire and nodded off to sleep.

When they woke up it was almost dark and the quietness all around them was a special kind of quietness, which Kitty knew meant only one thing. Creeping to the window she pulled back the curtain and looked out. Snow was falling, in big, white, ragged flakes.

"It's snowing, McGee," she whispered. Snow was always such a marvel to her that she felt it had to be talked about in a special voice. "It's a white Christmas. Isn't that fun? How long is it since that happened? It must be years."

"Must be," her friend muttered, giving a big yawn. "What a good thing we've done all our shopping. I don't fancy going out in that lot and slipping."

But Kitty was thinking exactly the opposite. She'd love to go out in the deep snow, walk about in the new, soft, miraculously white world, and watch the children tobogganing on the steep hill on the edge of town. But did children toboggan any more? She said, "There's one good thing about this snow, McGee. If Nicholas comes back we'll easily spot him."

"He's not coming back, dear, he's gone for good," McGee told her firmly. "And when Christmas is over we must get rid of all his things. They're cluttering up the place and looking at them is making you gloomy." They were making her gloomy too, though she wasn't going to admit it.

Nobody came to see them the day after Christmas, or the day after that, though Debbie phoned so many times asking for "news" that they rather wished she would stop. It just kept on snowing and the trees in the square became all blobby and big. It got so deep it came halfway up people's legs and slid down into their Wellington boots.

No one seemed to be going out much. Kitty sat by her window hoping she might see Timothy Joe all wrapped up warm, and his mummy and daddy pulling him round the square on a little sledge. But she didn't see him. What she did see, however, was something she had longed for even more than a sight of Debbie with Mr Moat (now his shop was open again) or of Timothy Joe, or of his brother or sister (for she was certain one existed).

What she saw, as the light faded on the day after the day after Christmas, was a gingery streak down in the garden in Golden Square. It was definitely ginger, and it was chasing its tail round and round. It was something that burned all warm and glowing against the unbroken, sparkling white of the snow. Nicholas used to chase his tail round and round just like that!

She didn't call McGee, she didn't even stop to put her coat on. She went straight downstairs and out into the square, wearing her thin indoor shoes and no coat, hat or gloves. She'd forgotten the key to the garden, so she squeezed through a space where two bits of the iron fence had broken away and started calling, "Nicholas, Nicholas, where are you?" But all was absolutely quiet.

There were lots of prints in the snow. Several animals with feet of assorted sizes had been there, some quite big, and she could see the tiny delicate traces of birds too. Calling Nicholas's name, she trudged up and down and round the garden, though with great difficulty because the snow was so deep and thick. She walked and called till her feet and legs were sodden with the melting snow, till her nose was like an icicle and her teeth chattering with cold. Only when she could bear the bitter air no longer did she turn, very reluctantly, for home.

Before she went to tell Miss McGee, she had a very hot bath with lots of bubbles, otherwise she feared she might get very bad flu, she had grown so cold. But Miss McGee, who had decided she might be getting flu herself, had already gone upstairs to bed and was snoring. So Kitty took up her position by the window again, and stared out over Golden Square, hoping for another sighting of the little gingery streak. When it got too dark to see she too went up to bed, where she fell asleep quite quickly and had lovely dreams of Nicholas chasing his tail round and round the garden.

Chapter Ten

First thing next morning, before Kitty could tell her about what she'd seen in the garden, Miss McGee dumped a cardboard box on the kitchen table.

"Right," she said. "One of us must take these to the Cat Rescue office. They've got hundreds of cats, they can use them. And the tins of cat food'll come in handy too."

Kitty watched miserably as things went into

the box: tins and packets of cat food, water bowls and food dishes, the ping-pong ball, the patchwork mouse and the spider with three legs. She had decided that it was just no good to tell Miss McGee that last night she'd seen what *might* have been a ginger cat chasing his tail down in the square but when she'd got there, he'd vanished. Her friend would say she was "seeing things", or dreaming.

Soon Miss McGee was sealing up the box with thick, brown sticky tape. "There," she said. "The sooner it's off the premises, the better we'll feel. Now, should we ring Reg to give one of us a lift down to Cat's Rescue?"

"No," Kitty answered. "I'll take it, I'd like some fresh air. I'll go on my bike. They've gritted the roads."

She was soon trundling off through the streets on her ancient bicycle, with the cardboard box wedged in the large wicker basket on the front. A thaw was coming now and the snow had turned a bit brown and slushy. As she went round Golden Square she called out "Nicholas!" because she *had* seen a ginger something chasing its tail. She knew, though, that it might have been a little fox. They did have foxes in Golden Square; they were very good at getting into dustbins and rubbish bags. Something had eaten a hole in one of their rubbish bags and had chewed hard on the remains of their crispy Christmas duck!

The Cat Rescue place was closed until New Year so Kitty, feeling much relieved, pedalled home again. She carried the box of Nicholas's things straight up into the attic and hid it in a corner under an old blanket. There was no need to tell McGee. If Nicholas didn't come back, she supposed they might have another cat, though her heart wasn't in this idea. A new cat could not replace the one they had lost.

Mr Plackett rang the doorbell and handed her a boring-looking brown envelope. "Thin post today," he muttered. "It's always the same after

Christmas. That cat of yours turned up yet?"

"No," said Kitty. "And we don't think he will, now. As a matter of fact I've just put all his stuff away in the attic."

"Good idea," said the postman. "You could advertise for a kitten I suppose, come the spring."

"I don't think so," murmured Kitty. "Not a young cat, anyhow. No, Mr Plackett, we have put away childish things." (It was one of her poetry sayings.)

Then she heard the telephone ringing behind her. "Goodbye, and a Happy New Year to you, when it comes," she called out rather sadly to the postman, before closing the door and walking down the hall to pick up the receiver.

A chirpy man's voice said, "I'm ringing about your notice. Has your cat come back?"

"No, no he hasn't, I'm afraid," Kitty replied, feeling suddenly quite breathless. "But, do you have any news of him?" She was thinking she might faint.

"Well, as a matter of fact, yes. I've just seen a cat that looks very like yours, sitting on a garden shed in Grendel Lane. Fluffy tail, you said in the description, small head, pretty little thing?"

"That sounds like him," Kitty said, speaking very, very quietly because she could hardly believe what the man was telling her. "But do give me your name, we are offering a reward." She might sound calm and in control to the man on the phone but, in reality, she had gone all wobbly at the knees. She was holding on to the edge of the telephone table to keep herself on her feet.

"Oh no," the man said. "That's quite all right. I'm glad I spotted him. But I'd go and fetch him right now, if I were you. Funny things, cats, moody creatures. He might run off."

Kitty would like to have explained to the caller that Nicholas did not have "moods", only it would have sounded ungrateful. He was a solid little cat, and he was always the same with them both. He was always loving, fun, and inquisitive, and full of jokes. It was only loud noises that frightened him and that wasn't a "mood". It was plain common sense to run away if you scented danger.

Having said "thank you" and having replaced the telephone, she went straight out into Golden Square, once again without a coat and in her thinnest shoes. The lovely snow had become a brown mush and by the time she got to the top of Grendel Lane her feet were sodden and she was making a squelch-squelch noise, as she trudged along.

There, on top of a garden shed just two doors down from Timothy Joe's house, curled up very neatly, like a chocolate without its frilly paper, was Nicholas. Or, if it wasn't Nicholas, then it was his double, "his spitting image", as some people might have said.

"Nicholas," she called out, but very softly, in case she frightened him.

Nicholas perked his ears up, raised his head from his furry chest and stared across at her. He didn't look very pleased to see Kitty, he was wearing his disapproving look, the look he gave her and Miss McGee if they removed him from the kitchen table where he liked to sit, but which, not being hygienic, was strictly against the rules.

"Nicholas," Kitty called again. "Where have you been? You've missed Christmas."

Nicholas went on staring at her coldly then stood up, stretched, sat down again and began to wash himself very elaborately. He took no further notice of her.

Kitty pondered for a moment. This was very odd. She had expected him to come leaping into her arms the minute he had heard her voice. If only she had thought to put a few of his favourite crunchy titbits into her pocket to tempt him off the roof of the shed.

She thought a bit harder. She had decided already that Nicholas must have been locked away somewhere, he was looking so terribly thin. That was it, he must have been accidentally shut in a disused garage or even a shed, like the one he was now sitting on. Perhaps a family had gone away for Christmas and shut him in their shed, not knowing he was there. The vet had told McGee that this sometimes happened to cats at Christmas time. That was it: he must have gone exploring. He was always going off on little secret expeditions.

She knew that she mustn't frighten him in any way. He must be very bewildered and scared already. He'd left home in the first place because he'd been frightened, and that was mainly her fault, because she'd burned the pudding and she and McGee had shouted at each other.

She could see a red phone box at the top of Grendel Lane and, digging down into the pocket of her skirt, she found some coins. With long, loping strides and not once taking her eyes off Nicholas, she walked quickly up to the box and went inside. She must ring McGee and ask her to come at once, with the cat basket.

But before she tapped out their home number, she decided to ring Mr Moat at his shop, in case it was one of Debbie's days for helping out. She was such a very sensible girl and Nicholas seemed to be in a rather strange mood. It might take three of them to entice him down from the roof of the shed.

Kitty was in luck! Mr Moat was back from his Christmas break, Mrs Springer had started her cleaning jobs again and Debbie, who was still on holiday from school, was indeed at the shop.

"She's a brilliant little worker," said Mr Moat. "She's cleaning all my shelves at the moment."

"Could I borrow her for half an hour?" asked Kitty. "We've found our cat; he's sitting on top of a shed in Grendel Lane. But he's in a bit of a funny mood and I think Debbie might be able to lure him off the roof."

"Of course," Mr Moat replied. "I'll shut the

shop for a few minutes and drop her off in the van. Could you meet her at the top of Grendel Lane?"

"I will," Kitty replied. "And one of us will bring her back, when Nicholas is safely home."

"Okey dokey," he said.

Only then did Kitty phone McGee. "Come at once," she ordered. "And bring the cat basket; it's still on top of the washing machine. I've found Nicholas; he's sitting on top of a shed in Grendel Lane, and I'm guarding him. Debbie's on her way to help us."

What a very good thing they had not taken the basket to the Cat Rescue place! If they had, it would be hidden in the attic by now, with all the other things that Kitty had smuggled back, and she would be in trouble with her friend, for not obeying orders. Worse, McGee could not possibly have climbed up the attic stairs, because of her bad legs.

"Thank you, dear St Jude, for finding

Nicholas," whispered Kitty, running back to the shed where Nicholas was still washing himself. (He had now turned his back on her completely!)

While she was waiting for McGee and Debbie, Kitty tried the handle of the gate to the garden with the shed and, to her surprise, it swung open with a rusty creak. The house was all boarded up and sad-looking. It had been for sale for ages but nobody seemed to want it. The old ladies had heard that this was because there were some nasty cracks in the back wall.

Kitty could now see these cracks quite clearly, and indeed, it looked as if, at any minute, the house might topple to the ground. No wonder nobody wanted to buy it! The garden was all overgrown and jungly, and the shed on which Nicholas sat was smothered in ivy. Kitty laid a hand on the ivy's glossy leaves.

"Dear Nicholas," she whispered softly, "I'm so glad we have found you, we've missed you so much. I'm sorry we shouted and made you run away." And when she said this Nicholas stood up, stretched, took a step towards her and rubbed his face against her outstretched hand.

She kept very still, holding her breath. It was vital not to scare him at this stage, so she just went on talking quietly as he crept towards her cautiously, inch by inch, and she tickled his ears, until, in a very few seconds, he was in her arms, purring and snuggling up as if they had never been parted.

"Yoo hoo!" called Debbie, from the top of Grendel Lane and she pelted down the cobbles.

She soon reached Kitty, who was cuddling Nicholas, and she had to skid to a halt, she was going so fast. The cheery "yoo hoo" and the sound of running feet, very clear and very echoey in the cold, frosty air, made the little cat stiffen with fright. His ears went flat against his head, he stared round wildly and began to struggle. If Kitty had not been holding him very tightly against her chest he would, she believed, have leaped out of her arms and run off again. He hated loud, unexpected noises. It was a horrid noise (McGee and Kitty quarrelling and throwing things) which had driven him away in the first place.

"Shh, shh, Debbie," she whispered, as the little girl came running up. "He's in a very nervous sort of mood. I suppose it's because he's been separated from us."

Debbie understood immediately and lowered her voice to a whisper, too. Then she began to stroke him with long, gentle strokes, all along his back. "You've got very bony, Nicholas," she said. "I can feel the knobbles all along your spine. Did you get shut in somewhere, you poor old thing?" And she laid her freckled cheek close to his fur.

Nicholas reached forward with his nose and rubbed himself against her. Then he began to unfold himself from Kitty's arms, reaching out towards Debbie, purring louder and louder. It was as if, with her, he felt extra specially safe. *How strange*, thought Kitty, letting the cat transfer himself from her arms to the little girl's. It was such a long time since Debbie had been to Golden Square, and yet Nicholas seemed to remember her very clearly, and to want her, even though he had always been a bit nervous of young people.

Debbie opened her arms wide to receive him, then cradled him against her coat. Nicholas closed his eyes and purred very softly, almost as if he was falling asleep. "He likes me," she said. But then, because she didn't want Kitty, her special "Granny Kitty", to be offended, she said quickly, "Perhaps it's because I'm little and you're big. He's little too and my gran says that animals often like children the best."

"I'm sure your gran is right," said Kitty, seeing, out of the corner of her eye, Miss McGee puffing along Grendel Lane with the cat basket.

All this happened just a week or so after Christmas, which was marmalade time, the time when those hard, bitter oranges you need to make it come into the shops. The old ladies were partial to marmalade. Miss McGee always made lots and lots, and she was in a hurry to get back to her kitchen where she had been busy chopping and squeezing oranges, when Kitty had made the phone call. In quite a short time, after giving Nicholas a very good stroke, and after tickling him behind his ears, she became very business-like.

She insisted on putting him into his basket, though Kitty was quite certain he would have preferred to be have been carried by Debbie. He hated the basket, it reminded him of having to go to the vet, of being prodded and poked and given injections and evil-tasting pills. But Debbie didn't say a word, Miss McGee was being so fierce.

"No!" she said, when Kitty protested. "Into the basket with him, this minute. There's a lot of traffic around, and we don't want any accidents. Come along, we've wasted enough time on this cat."

You would have thought Miss McGee was angry, she spoke so gruffly to Kitty, and she simply ignored Debbie, but the thing about Miss McGee was this: the gruffness was her way of saying she was glad Nicholas was back. Her private, happy, singing feelings about the safe return of their little cat were so strong that she had to hide them from view.

Her old friend understood this, and she put Nicholas firmly in his basket and shut the lid, ignoring his howls of protest. Debbie whispered, skipping along beside her and holding her hand, "I'm sure he would have been perfectly all right with me," but not loud enough for Miss McGee to hear.

Kitty walked home silently at her friend's side, with tears welling up in her eyes, but they were tears of happiness this time, and of gratefulness.

Chapter Eleven

Number 19 smelt strongly of oranges boiling in sugar. "I was going to ask you to do some chopping for me," grunted Miss McGee as she took off her coat, "but I suppose you want to spend some time with that cat of yours."

"McGee, dear, he belongs to both of us, you know that perfectly well," protested Kitty. "Aren't you glad to see him home?"

"Well, of course I'm glad, you great silly," came the reply in a voice that was almost a shout, but only because McGee was so pleased. Scooping up Nicholas she hugged him roughly. "Listen, you," she said, wagging her finger at him, "NO MORE DISAPPEARING TRICKS! AND NO MORE SQUEEZING UNDER GARAGES, or wherever you've been. You've had our Kitty worried to a frazzle. You know what they say, young man, 'Curiosity killed the cat.' Well, I think that you have been a very lucky one."

After this long speech (to which Nicholas had paid no attention, but during which he had struggled hard to get free) she dumped him on the kitchen floor. For a few seconds he stood quite still, looking from Miss McGee to Kitty then from Kitty to Debbie, then back again, as if he was trying to decide about something. Then he began to try and climb up Debbie's leg, sticking his claws into her jeans to get a good firm grip, as if he wasn't going to be parted from her again, not for one split second.

"Now I really must get on with my marmalade," announced Miss McGee. "Sort him out, will you, Kitty? I'll see you a bit later – I'm sure the two of you will manage without me. It's always such a help having you around, Debbie, and Nicholas obviously adores you. Just look at the silly creature!"

Kitty looked. Nicholas was now trying to drape himself round Debbie's neck, just as if he were a woolly winter scarf, and he was drooling like a baby, the front of her jersey was quite wet. Debbie decided she had better not stay too long, partly because she'd promised Uncle Ted that she wouldn't, but partly because she felt embarrassed about the way Nicholas was clinging to her. She could see that Kitty wanted to have some time on her own with him and she didn't want her to feel jealous. So after a short while she untangled herself from him, put him into the old lady's arms, and went back to the shop.

Miss McGee had now gone back to her marmalade making. Kitty could hear her humming as she bustled about with her oranges and lemons, her juice squeezer and her sharp little knife, and she didn't often hum, in fact she always said that humming got on her nerves. It meant she was most terribly pleased about Nicholas's safe return.

The next few hours passed in a dream for Kitty. She kept holding Nicholas very close, then far off, at arm's length, and inspecting him very carefully all over. He was extremely thin, and as light as a feather to hold, but this wasn't to be wondered at because, of course, he couldn't have eaten properly for days and days.

But why, when he had escaped from wherever he had been trapped, had he not come straight home? Why had he chosen to sit on that old shed on the far side of Golden Square, when he was so near home he could almost smell it? It

123

was a mystery. Another mystery was the way he'd wanted to go to Debbie. It was ages since she'd visited them in Golden Square, he surely couldn't remember her; and anyway, he had always preferred older people to children, who generally made a lot of noise and frightened him off.

A third mystery was how much he slept. The minute Kitty took her eyes off him, she found he had dozed off, like a small baby or a very old person. This wasn't like him at all. Nicholas was always tearing round the house, jumping on to tables (and being removed from them), crawling into paper bags, chewing things up, and wanting your full attention at all times because he was a cat who liked an audience. The old ladies had always compared life with him to life with the little children from Grendel School. You couldn't take your eyes off them for one minute, or they too were up to mischief.

But she supposed it might be quite normal, sleeping a lot after getting lost, or after being trapped in a dark place. Nicholas had obviously had a very bad shock. He was just being sensible, she supposed, and giving himself lots of rest to get over it.

Even so, all that afternoon she watched him carefully. It was his face that puzzled Kitty most. When she stared at it long and hard, it just didn't look quite like Nicholas, though, for the life of her, she couldn't say *how* it was different.

She got out her photograph albums, one of which was full of pictures of nothing but him, and she studied them very carefully, looking first at the photos, then at the real cat. Why was she worrying? All that was different was that he was thinner, and that would soon change because he was ravenous for food. Everything she gave him he gobbled up at once. He had the same small head, the same pretty face and the same plume-like tail as the cat in the photos. And neither she nor McGee had *ever* seen another cat quite like that. So it had to be Nicholas. Who else could it be unless, somewhere, he had an identical twin?

That evening, when the old ladies sat in their chairs with their bedtime drinks, Kitty confided her niggling worry to McGee. "Nonsense," her friend said stoutly. "I know it's a miracle, that he's come back after such a long time, but he has. We both said our prayers and our prayers were answered. You're worrying because you can't quite believe it. 'Can it be true?' is what you are saying. Well, it is true. Just look at him, and look at that tail. It's unique."

Kitty looked. Nicholas had taken up his favourite position and had draped himself round her neck.

"I've known lots of cats," Miss McGee went on, "but never a cat that did that, or one that got your attention by clambering up your legs, the way he does. Think of all those stockings you've ruined. You spoil that cat!"

Kitty smiled. "We both spoil him, McGee.

Don't think I don't see you making him those little extra snacks, when you're supposed to be doing the cooking."

Miss McGee blushed. "Well, a cat has to keep his strength up," she muttered.

Both old ladies were tired after the excitement of the day, and Miss McGee had chopped up dozens of oranges, too, so they went to bed early. Kitty always slept with her door shut, but Miss McGee always left hers open. And guess who came sneaking upstairs to join her, snuggling right down under the bedclothes and curling himself round her feet? Nicholas, of course.

Normally, she would have carried him down to the kitchen and shut him in. He had a very comfy basket of his own, by the cooker. But that night, she let him stay. It was cold and frosty outside and he made a nice hot-water bottle.

Miss McGee smiled as she fell asleep. Trying to sneak under her bedcovers on a winter's night

127

was something Nicholas had always tried to do, but it had hardly ever been permitted. She would tell Kitty he'd spent the night under her bedclothes, first thing in the morning, to stop her from worrying her silly head.

Well, of course it was Nicholas!

Chapter Twelve

The two old ladies got up early next morning, Kitty because she always did and Miss McGee because she was only halfway through her marmalade making, and she had to get on. She always made lots, to eat, to give away, and to sell for the church. Kitty wrote labels for the jars in her beautiful printing. *MISS McGEE'S MARMALADE* was all she put.

Nothing else was needed; the marmalade was famous.

Kitty woke much earlier than usual because of the sheer excitement of having Nicholas home again. While she was putting her shoes on, he appeared at her bedroom door and performed his familiar trick of trying to climb up her legs by sticking his claws in. When she picked him up for a cuddle, she could smell fish.

"Pooh! You've had a very fishy breakfast," she told him, and she put him down again hastily. He did seem to be extremely light: she could feel his bones through his fur. She wasn't going to tell Miss McGee off for giving him extra snacks. The sooner he got back to his normal weight the better.

She had planned to play with him, after she'd finished her jobs, but, the minute they reached the kitchen, he curled up in his basket and went to sleep. He showed no interest at all in his ping-pong ball, or his patchwork mouse, or his spider with three legs (Kitty had now confessed to Miss McGee that she had hidden them in the attic). Only two things got him out of his basket. One was food and the other was any unexpected noise. When the phone rang, or the doorbell, or one of the old ladies turned on the radio, Nicholas would leap out of his basket, put his ears back and make his whole body go flat. He did this several times that morning. Kitty, who was printing marmalade labels at one end of the kitchen table, was watching him very carefully.

"See that, McGee," she remarked. "That's not like our Nicholas."

"It's like our Nicholas *now*," Miss McGee reminded her. "Look, he's been missing for days and days, and we don't know what happened to him in that time. Something's obviously scared him stiff; he needs time to get his confidence back. He has to learn to trust us, Kitty, to trust us all over again."

Kitty sighed. "Yes, I'm sure you're right. We can't expect him to bounce back to normal in a jiffy, can we?" But when she peeped again at the thin, sleeping cat, which somehow didn't look quite right to her, the secret doubts she had grew.

Debbie phoned up twice, first to see how Nicholas was settling in now the old ladies had got him home again. Kitty told her about the niggling doubts, about how his face was just the same as before and yet how, in a way she could not explain, it was different. And Debbie rang her real gran and told her, and the real gran said "Ah now, that *is* mysterious..." And Debbie phoned Kitty back, and told *her*.

But Nicholas seemed delighted to be home again and made no attempt to escape, or go off on one of his adventures. Most of the time he just ate and slept.

That day passed quietly, and so did the next. Most of the time Nicholas was lazy and greedy and got away with doing exactly what he liked, including being permitted to sit on tables and snuggle down in beds. Though both these things were against the rules, the old ladies were letting him off. They agreed that it was important to show him how much they loved him, and that they were delighted he was home again. And anyhow, as Kitty used to say to her children at the Grendel School, "Rules are made to be broken" which was not exactly one of her poetry things, but still quite curious and interesting.

That year, Miss McGee had been rather ambitious about her marmalade making. She had decided to make one hundred jars. She called this her "personal best", a phrase she had heard on a radio programme. It was about a runner who wanted to win a gold medal in the Olympic Games. He had spoken of his "personal best" too, by which he had meant the very fastest he had ever run.

Kitty had not been asked to help with the boiling of the marmalade. She knew why, it was because she had burned the Christmas pudding. But she had printed one hundred labels for the jars and, when she had done the hundredth one, she felt exhausted. Her eyes ached, and her writing hand ached, and her back ached. "I'd like to go upstairs for a little sit down," she said to Miss McGee. "Is there anything else I can do?"

"No, thank you. I'll just get on with this lot, it's the very last batch. I've done ninety-four jars so far and this will make six more, and that will be a hundred."

"You are brilliant," Kitty said warmly, and she went off upstairs. To her great delight, Nicholas climbed out of his basket and followed her; when she was settled in her chair, the one that overlooked Golden Square, he jumped on to her lap, curled up and went to sleep. Kitty tickled his ears. This was very reassuring. It was the first time he'd got out of his basket by the cooker all day. It was much more like the old Nicholas. McGee was right. They must be more patient with him, and slowly he would return to his old self, after his great adventure.

She fell into a doze but was woken up by the telephone ringing down below. The minute he heard the bell, Nicholas leaped out of her lap and vanished underneath the settee, where she could see his beautiful amber eyes peering up at her.

"It's only the phone, Nicholas," she said gently. But the poor little cat looked terrified and the little worm of doubt began to gnaw once again, deep inside her.

The phone call was obviously for Miss McGee because, if Kitty had been wanted, she would have called up the stairs. That was their arrangement. After ten minutes it rang again and, fifteen minutes later, it rang for a third time. Kitty started to worry, and vaguely wondered what was wrong and whether she should go downstairs and see what had happened. They didn't get many telephone calls, and never three in a row. But she must have been more weary than she knew because, while she was still thinking about this, she fell asleep again.

Two things woke her up. The first was the acrid, unmistakable smell of burnt marmalade. The second was the touch of a hand upon her shoulder. She opened her eyes and blinked. Miss McGee was standing by her chair. Her face was all puffy and red and it rather looked as if she had been crying, which was most unusual. McGee *never* cried.

Kitty gripped the arms of the chair and made as if to stand up. "Oh, my goodness me, what a smell! Your marmalade, McGee..." She was still fuzzy from sleep, and slightly confused. She actually thought that it was she who had burned the marmalade. She said, "I'm terribly sorry, I nodded off. I can't have heard Big Time bleeping."

But Miss McGee had sat down beside her. "It's all right, it's my own fault, I let it burn. I had all these phone calls you see, to tell me that dear old Auntie Maggie had passed away. She would have been a hundred years old next week, and I was planning to make a cake, and to visit her. She sounded so well when we spoke on Christmas Day, it's such a shock." And although Miss McGee was not a crying sort of person, she allowed two little tears to roll down her cheeks.

Now Kitty wasn't just a kind friend, she was a thoughtful sort of lady in every way, and she did not say scornfully, as some people might have done, "'Pooh! No need to be sad about Auntie Maggie, she was nearly a hundred, after all, she's had a longer life than most." Instead, she whispered, "I am so sorry, McGee. She's been around for as long as you can remember and I know that you will miss her very much."

She put her thin hand on top of her friend's plump one, and they sat together in silence for a while, as the grey smoke from the burnt marmalade wafted round the room in thin wisps, and the terrified eyes of Nicholas peeped up at them from under the settee.

Kitty, too, had memories of Auntie Maggie. She had been McGee's mother's sister, and she had always lived on the family farm. She was a wonderful cook (like McGee), and she could ride a horse, and shear a sheep, and she had a sweet singing voice. She would sit by the fire in the old farm kitchen and sing songs to everybody about old country ways.

Miss McGee was thinking about all these things too, and hearing the sweet voice in her memory, and feeling just as if she were a little girl again, even though she herself was now nearly eighty years old.

She took out a handkerchief and dried her eyes. "Inside, you never stop feeling like a child, do you, dear?" she said to Kitty.

"No, dear, you never do," replied her friend. "Now then, what are we going to do about the marmalade? You really must reach your personal best you know."

"Oh, *that*," snorted Miss McGee, "I can't be

bothered with it any more. Anyway, all the marmalade oranges will have gone from the shops by now. They always get snapped up so quickly."

"I'll get you some," said Kitty. "I'll go right now and when I get back, I'll help you chop. You must reach your target of one hundred jars. Auntie Maggie would have wanted you to."

Miss McGee smiled. "I think you're right. If you could find a few more oranges, I could make one last batch. It'll take my mind off things."

Kitty stood up immediately. "I'll go right now," she said.

"You're a good friend to me," McGee told her.

"So are you, to me," Kitty replied. "So *that's* all right."

Chapter Thirteen

Miss McGee was right about the oranges, it seemed that every single shop had sold out. There must have been a real craze for marmalade making in Appleford that year.

First, Kitty went to the big supermarket, but they'd sold out, then she went to the little supermarket, and then to the medium-sized one, but they'd sold out too. Then she tried all the fruit and vegetable shops in the main shopping street of the town, but it was always the same story, "Sorry, love, we did have some, but they've all gone now, and we won't be getting any more. It's always a short season, for marmalade oranges."

She tramped in and out of shops until her feet were aching. Finally, having quite given up, she stopped at a little café for a cup of tea and a sticky bun before setting off for home again. She needed the bun to give her some energy for the walk back home. She was the very last customer at the café. As she went through the door, the lady turned the OPEN sign to CLOSED. That meant the shops would be shutting, too, so there was no chance of finding oranges now.

She decided to walk home a different way from usual, through Albert Park. She was tired of walking, but even more tired of hard pavements; she wanted to see some grass, perhaps even feel it, under her feet. The snow had melted now and had left lots of nasty, brown mud behind. The paths were sticky with it and it clung to the soles of her shoes in big lumps. Walking along was quite difficult.

The first green shoots of the year were already pushing up through the grass and, under the trees, she saw thick carpets of aconite flowers, looking like scatterings of little yellow stars. There were a few clumps of snowdrops, too, and, as she passed a Daphne bush, her nostrils were filled with the sweet scent of its pink flowers. But, though Kitty's heart always filled with happiness at these faithful signs of nature, these promises that spring would come again, her spirit was troubled. All felt strangely grey to her. The sky was grey and the pond in the middle of the park was grey. Even the swans looked a bit grubby and grey, that bleak January afternoon.

Kitty knew this grey feeling was about Nicholas. All the time she had been trying to find oranges to buy, she had kept noticing cats (there were dozens of cats in Appleford). Quite a few had been ginger ones, and a couple had looked a bit like Nicholas, cats that could well have been a brother or a sister to him, or a first cousin. What was giving Kitty this unpleasant grey feeling was the worry, deep down, that the cat she had lured off the roof of the shed was not Nicholas at all, but another cat exactly like him; not alike merely to look at, but in the way he behaved. After all, Debbie's real gran, who knew all about animals, had said that Kitty's doubts about Nicholas's face, which sometimes seemed not to be *his* face, had said it was "very mysterious indeed".

She had pored and pored over her cat photographs but couldn't decide why she was feeling so uncertain. Most of the time she was confident that it was indeed Nicholas, and that he was just needing time to get back to his old self. But now and again, these funny feelings of doubt swept over her, like washes of cold water.

She was nearly back at Golden Square when she noticed that Mr Moat's shop was still open. He worked very hard, opening early and closing late, for the convenience of his customers. Indeed, over the doorway it said **MOAT'S CONVENIENCE STORE** in curvy letters. People said he was very rich but Kitty wasn't sure about that. He always wore very old clothes and had a rusty delivery van.

She hadn't tried his shop for oranges because it didn't sell fruit and vegetables. But, guess what? Out on the pavement, next to some buckets and brushes, was a large brown cardboard box and a notice that said "Best Marmalade Oranges". Kitty went straight inside.

"I've been all over town," she told the shopkeeper, "but everybody has sold out. I've walked my legs off this afternoon, looking for oranges. I never thought of trying you."

"New line," Mr Moat told her. "Everyone's

making their own marmalade this year, they're all going organic. How many do you want, Miss Kitty?"

"Er, ten," she told him. "Miss McGee said to buy ten. She has a few more jars to make; she burned the last lot. She received a sad telephone call to tell her that her Auntie Maggie had died, and she got distracted. She is going for a personal best this year of one hundred jars."

Mr Moat put the oranges in a brown paper bag and Kitty gave him some money. "You must be so pleased that that cat of yours has come back," he said. "I've only just remembered, your notice is still in my window. I'd better take it out. Is that OK?"

Kitty hesitated then gave him rather a flat little smile. "Er, yes, he's back. Do remove it."

The shopkeeper peered at her curiously. "You don't seem awfully sure about this, Miss Kitty," he murmured.

"Er, yes, yes. Remove it. He's definitely back,

only he's — how can I put this — well, it seems to me that he is much changed."

Mr Moat shrugged. "Oh, he'll come round. He's probably had a bit of a shock. Our Debbie said he was ever so pleased to see her. She was a little bit embarrassed about it, between you and me."

"Oh she mustn't be, Mr Moat," Kitty said warmly. "It was sweet, he couldn't get enough of her; in fact, he pined a little bit when she went home. It was so strange because he's always been a bit nervous of children, even children like Debbie who know how to handle him. Anyhow, I don't know where he went off to, but he's home now. It's just that, as I say, there's something different about him, though I couldn't explain exactly what it is."

"He'll be OK," the shopkeeper assured her. "You know how it is, a pretty cat like that, someone probably nicked him, gave him to their kid for Christmas, then changed their mind and dumped him somewhere. It's cruel, what some people get up to. You know what they say, 'A pet's not just for Christmas, it's for life'."

Kitty put the bag of oranges into her shopping bag and set off for home, along Grendel Lane where the closed-down school was. It was a slightly longer route than her normal one, but she liked walking past the school, even though it was all boarded up and silent. It reminded her of happy times.

She walked past Timothy Joe's garden gate and she walked past the garden gate of the toppling-over house, where she had found Nicholas sitting on the shed, and she walked past the red telephone box from which she had phoned McGee.

Next to this phone box was a lamppost, the old-fashioned kind which, when she and McGee were little girls, would have been switched on by the lamplighter man. It was nearly dark now and the lamp was on, spreading a circle of soft yellow light on the ground at her feet.

Then she noticed something. A notice had been fixed to the lamppost with thick, brown sticky tape. It was written in wobbly, child-like print and it said:

MISSING: GINGER CAT,
VERY PRETTY. SMALL
HEAD. PLUME-LIKE TAIL.
ANSWERS TO THE NAME
"FLUFFY". IF YOU SEE HIM
PLEASE PHONE
APPLEFORD 77198.

Very slowly, Kitty put down her shopping bag and read the notice several times. It was stuck to the very same lamppost on which they had stuck their "Nicholas" notice, after he had disappeared. When she was certain that she could remember what it said, she dug in her pocket and found a stub of pencil. She tore off a corner of the brown paper bag that contained McGee's oranges and wrote the phone number on it. Then she walked home, just as quickly as she could.

Chapter Fourteen

Miss McGee was in the kitchen waiting for her ten oranges. The pan she had burned had been scrubbed clean, and dried, and sat on the table, all ready for the boiling. She had weighed out the sugar on her scales with their shiny brass weights. She had counted out six jars and polished them. But she had also prepared a tray of tea for poor, worn-out Kitty. She had baked home-made scones, and there was jam to put on top of them, and even a little dish of thick cream.

"I thought we might give Nicholas a little spoonful, as a treat," she said. "He so loves cream."

"It isn't Nicholas," Kitty told her in a very flat voice. "I knew it wasn't, I knew all along, but you wouldn't listen to me." She told Miss McGee all about the "missing Fluffy" notice in Grendel Lane. When she'd finished she said, with a ghost of a smile, "But I did find you some oranges, at Mr Moat's, so there's a bright side to everything," and she dumped her brown paper bag on the table.

Miss McGee put the kettle on and bustled about. She took no notice whatsoever of the oranges, Kitty was looking much too crestfallen. Instead she said, "Now we mustn't do anything in a hurry, dear. For all we know, it's just... what do people call it these days? Yes, I know, it's just a fluke. There may well be some identical twin cats in Appleford, there may even be triplets, lots of

150

pretty little ginger cats, all looking exactly alike. I really think we must take our time about this, Kitty, and not do anything rash. That cat of ours looks exactly like Nicholas to me, and he's already ruined two lots of good stockings by trying to climb into your arms. He's a shocker."

"McGee, it isn't Nicholas, it's a Nicholas look-alike, we've catnapped him by mistake, and I'm taking him back to his rightful owners. Where is he?"

"Still hiding under your settee, as far as I know. He won't come out. I've tried and tried."

"There you are. I'm right. The real Nicholas would have come out by now, you know that perfectly well."

"All right, if you insist, dear. Make your phone call. But I expect they'll have got their own cat back by now, and if so, we can all rest easy. Now listen, why don't you have a cup of tea first, before you ring these people? And it's a pity not to eat the scones while they're still warm."

"*No*," said Kitty firmly. "I must do it now," and she marched off into the hall, where the telephone was, shutting the kitchen door behind her.

The truth was that she was in the grip of a most terrible temptation, and the nature of the temptation was this: they could easily keep Not Nicholas, nobody would know. It was true that he was still scared of things, but on the whole he was settling in very well, and the owners of Fluffy need never know that Kitty and Miss McGee had adopted him. In time they would get another cat.

But Kitty was brave, braveness was in her blood, the braveness of her father who had fought in war campaigns. Besides, she had taught her children at Grendel School that they must try to be brave and, above all, truthful, and now she had to set a good example, even though there was nobody around to see. On her own, in the hall, Kitty squared her shoulders and picked up the telephone.

It rang three times then a woman's voice said, "77198, Mary Atkinson speaking."

For a moment, Kitty did not reply. She couldn't. She was trying very hard to speak, but something was stopping the words coming out, something that seemed to be stuck in her throat, something that felt like a horrible lump of gristly meat. Mary Atkinson had got to be Timothy Joe's mother!

The crisp, rather high-pitched voice was the same voice that Kitty had heard shouting at Timothy Joe, down in the garden. Furthermore, Timothy Joe lived just two doors away from the toppling-over house where she had found Not Nicholas on the shed. This lady was the "monster" with the fair hair and the cherry-red raincoat, the lady who always seemed so cross and in a hurry, and did not want to be friendly.

"Hello?" said the voice, even more crisply. "Who is that? Can you hear me?"

"Yes... yes..." stammered poor Kitty at last.

"My name is Kitty and I've just seen your notice, the one about the missing cat called Fluffy. I live at Number 19 with my friend Miss McGee. The fact is we... I... we have your cat here. Ours vanished, and we put up some notices, and somebody phoned me to say they'd found him and we brought him here, to live with us. We really did think he was ours. I shall come straight over with him," and, without waiting for Mrs Atkinson to reply, she replaced the telephone.

Then, very unexpectedly, her bravery began to seep away, and to seep away quite fast. She felt so foolish, even a tiny bit wicked. She and McGee, but mainly she, had actually *stolen* somebody else's cat, and they were old ladies. It must look terrible to the outside world. She needed an ally, someone to go with her to the Atkinsons and stick up for her if they got cross and began to shout, a person who could explain how easily one cat might be mistaken for another. The person she needed was Debbie.

Without consulting McGee, who would perhaps have said she was silly, she rang Mrs Springer on her mobile and this time she got an answer. "Yes," said Mrs Springer, "Debbie's right here. She's not doing much, just watching telly."

Kitty took a very deep breath then blurted out her story, all in a rush. "The thing is, Mrs Springer," she explained, "we've accidentally captured someone else's cat. Debbie was such a help when we were searching. The little creature we brought home looks exactly like Nicholas, and he's settled down really well. *But* I'm afraid I've just spotted a notice saying that a ginger cat's gone missing and I've just got to take ours back, in case it's theirs. The lady of the house is a bit fierce though; I suspect they've got some family trouble. If I could borrow Debbie for an hour, to help me with Nicholas – I mean Fluffy – I know it would help.

Debbie's mum interrupted. "Fierce, did you say? It's not Mrs Atkinson, is it?"

"Yes, it is," replied Kitty. "Do you know her?"

"Not exactly, but there *has* been trouble there. I went after a job when they moved in, but I could never get hold of anybody, and when I did she gave me very short shrift, told me to ring back at a more convenient time. Well, I didn't bother. Once bitten, twice shy, that's what I say."

"So could I borrow Debbie, then? I'll come in a taxi and I'll bring her straight home afterwards."

"Of course you can, but don't bother coming all the way out here," said Mrs Springer. "I've got to see Ted today anyway. I'll bring Debbie round. I could even come with you."

Kitty hung up the phone feeling very relieved. She now had not one, but TWO people to help her.

A short time later they were all standing on the doorstep of Number 26 Golden Square. Not Nicholas, whom they must now think of as

Fluffy, had, indeed, been hiding in Kitty's sitting room, but he had plucked up a little courage and moved from his place under the settee to a different one under a chair. Debbie had spent ages patiently coaxing him out of hiding but Kitty, who was now feeling more and more foolish about her mistake, had scooped him up without any ceremony and plonked him in the wicker cat basket where he cowered, mewing rather pitifully.

Kitty had strange, angry feelings now and she knew she was taking these feelings out on poor Fluffy. It was because she was so disappointed at not having the real Nicholas home again. He must still be lost somewhere, or trapped, or dead. She'd thought all along that Fluffy might not be Nicholas, and one clue to this curious doubt of hers had been that, after his return, she had not been quite able to love him as before. The "feel" of this cat had been wrong to Kitty. It wasn't the look, it was the feel.

Another clue had been the way he had preferred Debbie's company to hers. The real Nicholas had much preferred quiet old ladies to lively, bouncing children. So, the sooner his rightful owners got Fluffy back, the better for everybody.

She pressed the Atkinsons' doorbell firmly, and the door opened at once, so "at once", that Timothy Joe's mother must surely have been standing right behind it. Now Kitty had planned simply to hand over the cat, then to leave immediately. They could return the basket any old time, or the Atkinsons could keep it. She was going to explain how she and McGee wouldn't be needing a cat basket any more. She had a little speech all prepared, to this effect.

But to her surprise, Timothy Joe's mother didn't yell "How terrible of you, to steal another person's cat in broad daylight!" which was what poor Kitty had expected from someone who had always seemed to be shouting and yelling. Instead, as soon as Mrs Atkinson opened the door, she said,

"I am so sorry about this," in a very kind way and then she said, looking down, "and I'm sorry, er..."

"Debbie," said Debbie. "I helped with Fluffy, when we saw him on the shed. It was my fault too, that we made the mistake," and for the very first time since this adventure had started, she found that she couldn't speak and very much wanted to cry, not for herself, but for Granny Kitty, who obviously loved Nicholas so much.

As Timothy Joe's mother ushered Kitty and Debbie inside, Mrs Springer slipped away quietly to see her brother at his shop. She could see that Mrs Atkinson was very nice indeed and not at all fierce.

Kitty was so flabbergasted at the very kind way Mrs Atkinson had spoken to them, that her knees did their usual trick of going all wobbly on her. Without asking permission, she sank down on to the nearest chair. Debbie took up a position just behind her and held her hand. Timothy Joe's mother took a seat in the chair beside her and said, "Are you feeling all right, Kitty? You've gone very pale. Can I bring you a drink of water?"

Kitty gulped. "No, I'm quite all right, thank you. If you would kindly confirm that the cat in the basket is Fluffy, then I'll be off. I feel absolutely awful about this. Whatever must you think of us, stealing someone else's cat?"

Mary Atkinson said nothing, but opened the lid of the basket a couple of inches, and peeped inside. Then she reached down, took out Not Nicholas, and placed him very firmly on her lap. He looked scared, his eyes were white and wild, and his ears had gone completely flat against his head. For a few seconds he struggled to get free but Mrs Atkinson spoke soft, soothing words to him, and stroked his back with long strokes, and very soon he stopped wriggling and seemed perfectly content to be in her arms. Debbie stretched out a hand and tickled him too, and Not Nicholas, alias Fluffy, started to purr deeply, like a little engine.

Kitty was impressed. "You obviously know how to handle animals," she said. "He has faith in you. He's calmed down."

"My father was a vet," said Timothy Joe's mother. "Our house was always full of animals and I used to help him. My brother Tom's a vet too, in fact, he's going to open a surgery soon, in this town. I suppose it's in our blood, handling animals. But it looks to me as if Debbie here could be a good vet. Fluffy's obviously very happy to have her around. Is she your granddaughter?"

"No," Kitty replied. "But if I *had* a granddaughter, I'd like one exactly like Debbie."

"She's my extra granny," Debbie announced. "I've got an official one, she lives in Blackpool. Kitty's my extra one. Miss McGee's an extra one too. I've got three grannies."

Mrs Atkinson had now opened the cat's mouth very wide, as if she wanted to give him a pill. "Look," she said to Kitty. "Look on the roof of his mouth. Can you see those three little black spots?"

Kitty adjusted her spectacles and peered into the little pink cavern. "My goodness me, well I never," she exclaimed.

"Fluffy was born with little spots like that," Timothy Joe's mother explained. "Now you wouldn't know, would you, whether *your* cat has spots in his mouth? If he hasn't, then that's one way of telling them apart. It will tell us whether this cat is Fluffy and not – what is your cat called…?"

"Nicholas," Kitty told her. "His name is Nicholas."

"Nicholas," repeated Mrs Atkinson. "That's a pretty name!"

"Yes, isn't it? He's a pretty cat. 'A pretty name for a pretty cat' was what my friend McGee said, when we got him as a kitten. She chose it. She's good at names."

"But you wouldn't know, would you, whether

Nicholas has three little spots like this, inside his mouth?"

"No, I'm afraid I wouldn't, and nor would McGee. He's a shocker, when it comes to swallowing pills. We always have to get the vet to do it." And of course, that was another thing. This cat had obligingly opened his mouth, the minute Mrs Atkinson had wanted him to, whereas Nicholas would have absolutely refused. Here was more proof that the cat on the roof was Fluffy, not that Kitty needed any proof now.

"Have you ever noticed the inside of Nicholas's mouth, Debbie?" asked Kitty. "Does it have three little black spots inside?"

Debbie knew perfectly well that it had not. Nicholas had been forever giving great big yawns, she had often teased him about it, and she'd had lots of chances to look at the inside of his mouth. But she terribly wanted Fluffy to be Nicholas so they could take him home again and wait for the real Fluffy to turn up. She swallowed hard and said vaguely, "Dunno, couldn't rightly say, one way or the other, Granny Kitty!"

The old lady squeezed her hand.

"What a pity. How else can we be sure?" said Timothy Joe's mother, very solemnly. Even if she knew perfectly well that she was holding Fluffy, she was trying to let Kitty down gently, which was kind of her, though misguided. All poor Kitty wanted now was to *go home* and have a good cry, in private.

Suddenly, she remembered something and felt in her pocket. "I have a photo of Nicholas with me. Here, take a look. I'm sure you can see how we made our mistake."

Mrs Atkinson took the photo and studied it carefully. "Oh, well this is unbelievable!" she exclaimed. "They really are identical, aren't they? It's amazing, but—" and suddenly, she grew thoughtful. "Ah, but there is a difference. The cat on this photo, Nicholas, has a wee patch of white fur just under his chin, whereas Fluffy here is ginger all over. Every speck of him is ginger, there's not a single white hair. See for yourself."

Kitty looked carefully at Fluffy, then at her photograph. "You're right," she said, after quite a long pause. "There is a little patch, though it's only tiny. It was quite big when he was a kitten, but now it's almost disappeared. I'd quite forgotten that patch. My friend McGee used to say that he looked as if he'd dipped his chin in the cream. He adores cream, you see – I mean *adored*." From now on, she was going to speak in the past tense about Nicholas. Bringing Fluffy back to his rightful owners really did feel like the official end of something. McGee had already drawn a line under the Nicholas affair and now Kitty knew that she was right. They must draw a double line and they must RULE OFF.

Debbie said in a sad little whisper, knowing now that they really had captured the wrong cat, "I remember that little patch of white, Gran."

"Right," Kitty said in a firm voice, getting up from her chair. "I can only apologise once again for our awful mistake. I do hope you won't think too badly of us, kidnapping your poor cat. We would like to be good neighbours but this is a very bad start."

"Not at all," said Mrs Atkinson, also getting to her feet, "I can quite see how you made the mistake. They are so alike, it's uncanny. But before you go, please come and meet Annie. She printed the notices we stuck up round the square. She insisted on making them all herself, because Fluffy is her cat. He was her coming home present. We got him from the Cat Rescue place."

Who was Annie? Kitty knew all about Timothy Joe, but not about anyone called Annie. Might it be that funny little lady with the duster who had refused to let her in last time she had visited Number 26? Might it be a very ancient auntie? In a daze, she allowed Mrs Atkinson to lead her and Debbie along the hallway, and into a room at the front of the house, wondering who on earth this new, extra person might be.

Chapter Fifteen

The room she was taken into was very like Kitty's own sitting room, except that it was bigger, and had two windows instead of one. Like her room, it overlooked Golden Square. There, in one of these windows, was a beautiful rocking horse, all glossy black. The carpet was littered with toys and books and on a big sofa, surrounded by dolls and teddies, all tucked up warmly in a tartan rug, was a small, very white-faced girl. She had golden curls and a face like Timothy Joe. In fact, had she not been a bit older, and a girl, she might have *been* Timothy Joe!

Debbie stood spellbound on the threshold, looking at the beautiful toys and the lovely soft rug in which the pale-faced girl was swaddled, longing to climb on to the rocking horse's back, to plait its mane and stroke it. How different this flat was from the small, modern sitting room in their flat. Mum didn't have much money for expensive things, it was all quite bare where she lived.

Kitty stared hard at the little girl on the sofa, and before she could stop herself, she cried out, "I knew it. You must be Timothy Joe's sister. I knew there was more than one child, because I saw two bicycles, the day you moved in."

"Annie has been very, very ill, Kitty," explained Mrs Atkinson. "She fell ill just before we moved into this house, and she was rushed into hospital. That's why I have been such a bad neighbour, I'm afraid, and so bad-tempered when I met you in the square. Her daddy and I have spent all our time at her bedside and Timothy Joe has been rather neglected. So many different people have had to look after him, poor mite. But, as you see, Annie is safe and well again, and very soon you'll be running around, won't you, Annie, and playing with Timothy Joe, down in the square? Now, before Granny Kitty and Debbie go home, I have a present for you," and without saying any more, she went out of the room.

Kitty sat down on the edge of the sofa and Debbie sat beside her. She felt rather shy of Annie, and sorry for her. She wanted her to be able to get up off the sofa and run around. Annie inspected them both silently, with huge brown eyes.

"It was I who brought the present," Kitty said softly. "Fluffy's back. I think your mummy must have gone to fetch him," and as she said this, Mrs Atkinson came back into the room carrying the cat basket. "Isn't that typical of cats!" she exclaimed. "He refuses to come out of the basket now, he's snuggled right down!"

Debbie whispered soft, cajoling words into the basket and after a few seconds Fluffy poked his head out and rubbed it against her hand. Very carefully, and not rushing, she scooped him up and put him gently down on top of the tartan rug, very close to Annie.

Kitty watched. She understood now why the cat had preferred Debbie to her. Fluffy's real owner was a little girl, someone not many years younger than Debbie.

"Fluffy!" squealed Annie, and she sat straight up and stretched out her arms. In spite of the loud squeal, the cat went up to her at once and purred and slobbered and gave her lots of wet kisses. Then he curled up in a tight ball on her tummy while Annie stroked and stroked him. "I knew you'd come back," she said. "But where on earth have you been, you naughty little cat? I've been so worried about you."

Kitty opened her mouth to explain. "I'm sorry to have to confess…" she began. But Mrs Atkinson frowned across at her and shook her head, as if to say, "There's no need to explain about taking him home by mistake." She just said briskly, "Granny Kitty read your notice in Grendel Lane, and, well, here he is. All's well that ends well."

"Next time you come," she said to Kitty, when they were back in the hall, "You must meet Timothy Joe too. He's having a little nap and I don't want to wake him up, it makes him grumpy. We are still having to keep Annie very quiet, of course. She's had…" and she reeled off the long Latin name of the rare and horrible illness which Annie had suffered from, an illness from which, it seemed, she had very nearly died.

Kitty decided she would have to repeat the name of the illness to herself all the way home, so that she could tell McGee, who used to be a children's nurse and would know all about it. She said, "What a worrying time it must have been for you, Mrs Atkinson, and just as you were moving house."

"Yes. I shall be so glad to get back to normal bedtimes again, and to normal mealtimes. I was beginning to think I had started to look like a pizza. That's what we ordered you see, when we got home from the hospital. It was nothing but takeaway food for ages. We've been living on pizzas and curries and fish and chips. We've had to eat at such funny times of the day and night because we never knew what was going to happen to Annie. One of us was always at the hospital and the other was coping with Timothy Joe. You must have thought we were the most unfriendly people."

"Not at all," murmured Kitty, though not quite truthfully. (But, how could she say, "Yes, that's exactly what we thought!" Sometimes, one had to tell a very tiny white lie, in order to spare people's feelings.)

Everything was fitting together now like a

jigsaw puzzle. The crossness of Mrs Atkinson, her husband's very worried look, all that rushing about and ordering pizzas at ten o'clock in the morning. And there was that day in the square too, when she'd thought Timothy Joe was playing trains. "Chu, chu, chu," he'd been calling. But it wasn't a train noise, it was his special call for Fluffy, who had got out and was hiding in the bushes. Mrs Atkinson had explained this to her, as they stood talking on the doorstep. What a muddle it all was!

A bit of her was very sad. If only she and McGee had known that Annie was so ill, and the parents so worried, they could have helped. At the very least they could have looked after Timothy Joe. Little children had always loved coming to the house of Kitty and Miss McGee. But since Debbie and her mum had gone to live in the Flats, no children had been to visit for a very long time

As they said goodbye Mrs Atkinson told her,

"My brother Tom, the vet, is coming to live in Golden Square. He's bought that house with the alarming cracks, two doors down. He got it cheap but he knows a very good builder who's going to fix it up for him. And Tom has *six* children so I'm afraid there's going to be an awful lot of noise, from now on, round here. There won't be a dull moment! I expect you'll get tired of us."

"Not at all," said Kitty. "It's wonderful news, we'll love it. We are becoming very old and boring, and set in our ways. We may have lost one cat but we've gained eight children. That can't be bad. I am going home this minute, to tell my friend McGee."

She left the cat basket behind, "accidentally-on-purpose". It didn't matter now, she didn't want to get another cat. She had lovely memories of Nicholas and those must suffice. She would ring Mary Atkinson up tomorrow and tell her to keep it, or she could give it to brother Tom, the vet. A vet could never have too many cat baskets and there was soon to be a vet's surgery in Golden Square.

But first thing next day, when they had only just got up and were still in their dressing gowns, the doorbell rang. Kitty went downstairs and opened the door but nobody was standing on the step. There was only a cat basket, and two bunches of flowers labelled "Granny Kitty" and "Granny McGee", a box of chocolate kittens for Debbie and a letter from Annie which said:

THANK YOU FOR
BRINGING BACK FLUFFY.
I AM SORRY ABOUT
NICHOLAS. MUMMY TOLD
ME HE WAS LOST. IF
YOU WANT, I WILL MAKE
NOTICES AND WE WILL
STICK THEM UP. LOVE
FROM ANNIE AND
TIMOTHY JOE. xxx

Chapter Sixteen

Later that morning, Kitty climbed on to her bicycle and set off to see the Cat Rescue people, with all Nicholas's things. This time the office was open. She explained that they'd lost their cat, but not that they'd stolen somebody else's. That part of the story was too embarrassing, and too awful.

The lady in the office was very sympathetic

and said how sorry she was that Nicholas had vanished. She seemed very unwilling to accept his toys, or his bowls, or his uneaten tins of cat food.

"Listen," she advised, "don't rush into this. We have lots of cats that need good homes; why don't you have one of ours? If you wait, I can fetch some for you to look at; we have plenty of lovely cats to choose from."

"No thank you," said Kitty very firmly. "No more cats for us. Good morning," and she cycled home, and the two old ladies picked up their lives again, and got on with them.

Most days, they saw the Atkinsons coming and going in the square. Timothy Joe often played outside, with his mother or his father, or with the helper whose name was Mina. And sometimes Annie came to the window and watched. She still looked very pale and thin. They saw Fluffy, too. He sometimes followed Timothy Joe into the square, and played with him and chased his tail. Kitty would turn away from the window when she saw this; it made her too sad.

They did not actually speak to the Atkinsons again until they saw them one day at church. It was the time of Epiphany, a couple of weeks after Christmas, when people remember the story of the Three Wise Men, who brought presents to Jesus of gold, and frankincense, and myrrh.

There was always a special service on that day and the choir sang special things; there were lots of candles and a sweet-smelling mistiness in the air, and it was beautiful. The Atkinsons were all there, including Annie, and they said "Hello" again, to Kitty, and "Hello" for the first time, to Miss McGee, and of course they asked if there was any news of Nicholas.

"Alas, no," Miss McGee told them, but Kitty found that she could not speak at all because what she actually wanted to do was to cry, and she mustn't do that, not in front of Annie and Timothy Joe. For Annie was five and Timothy Joe was three and Kitty, even though she still rode a bicycle, was seventy-six and a half.

This wanting to cry made her realise that, though she had tried very hard to draw a thick DOUBLE line under the Nicholas affair, she had not succeeded. So, before she left the church she said a very special prayer to St Jude, and this is how it went:

"Dear St Jude, saint of hopeless things and hopeless people, I know I am being hopeless, but I can't seem to forget about Nicholas. I still miss him very much. Please help me to forget about him now, and to resume my normal life, and to do my jobs, as I must. In the name of the Father, and of the Son, and of the Holy Spirit, Amen."

But she knew the prayer hadn't worked, and that she was still worrying about him, because now she found that she couldn't go to sleep at night. In fact, she slept so badly that she actually wondered if she should go and visit the doctor and get some pills.

But Kitty didn't like taking pills. In that respect she was exactly like Nicholas, so she decided not to visit the doctor. She told herself firmly that she would just have to put up with this not sleeping, until things changed for the better. (She had discovered that everything changed in the end, if you waited long enough.)

One night, two weeks after Epiphany, she was lying awake as usual and feeling very grumpy, when she suddenly remembered something her mother had told her when she was a little girl. "If you can't get to sleep, Katherine Elizabeth," (for that was Kitty's full and proper name) "think of the most beautiful thing in the world, and concentrate on that, and the chances are you will go to sleep in no time."

Kitty closed her eyes and thought hard, and into her head floated a picture of the Three Wise Men holding out their gifts of gold, frankincense and myrrh. Somewhere in the background was a manger full of hay, with Baby Jesus in it, and Mary and Joseph, and all the animals; and sitting at Mary's feet was a little ginger cat. He'd come to worship the special baby too. Kitty didn't get close enough in the dream to decide whether the cat was Nicholas, or Fluffy, or another cat that looked a bit like them, because her mother's advice had done the trick and she had fallen fast asleep.

When she woke up, it was four in the morning. Kitty knew this because, as she opened her eyes, she heard a clock somewhere in the town strike four times. Suddenly, for no reason she could fathom, she had found that she was wide awake and sitting up in bed. Something was scratching frantically at her bedroom door and whatever it was, was making a very loud howling noise.

Kitty sat bolt upright and switched on her bedside light. She listened carefully and shouted,

"Stoppit!" very loudly, but the howling and the scratching just carried on, getting more and more frantic.

She did nothing at first because, after all, the noise could have been a burglar – someone pretending he was a wild animal that had escaped from a zoo. (She was not thinking very clearly. A burglar would have surely kept as quiet as possible, if he'd come in to steal things.) But this did not occur to her at the time, nor did it occur to her that she was in danger, because she got straight out of bed, marched across the carpet, flung open the door and barked crossly into the darkness, "What on earth do you think you're doing, waking up the household?" And as she said this something leaped into her arms, and slobbered and purred, and clung on for dear life with every one of his claws, as if nothing, but NOTHING would part him from Kitty, ever again.

Chapter Seventeen

It was a long, long time before she could bring herself to let Nicholas creep out of her arms. He was so thin, she feared he might melt away when she wasn't looking. His fur was all matted and a little piece of skin had been bitten out of his left ear. It was raining, she could hear it beating against the windows, and his fur was quite sodden with water. When, reluctantly, he allowed her to put him down (only so that she could have a good look at him), he walked slowly across the bedspread, making big muddy pawmarks all over it. Kitty didn't care a bit. He was back, horribly thin, with a chunk out of his ear, and all wet and dirty and scruffy, but it was Nicholas, of this fact she had no doubt at all.

How could she be so sure, after the mistake about Fluffy? It wasn't the tiny white patch under his chin or the fact that, when she opened his mouth (the first time he had ever allowed her to), there were no little black spots. It was what, afterwards, she could only call "the Nicholas-ness of Nicholas". It was the *feel*.

He felt like Nicholas and he smelt like Nicholas, even though, unless he'd been eating fish, he didn't usually smell of anything much. It was hard to explain how she knew, she just felt it, in those bones of hers, the bones which had never let her down in the past.

Now, Kitty had never been married, and

neither had Miss McGee, and they had no children. McGee had been about to marry, once, but her sweetheart, who was a soldier, had been killed in a battle. He had been a brave man, like Kitty's father. When people asked Kitty why she had no husband she simply said, "Well, I have very long legs and I used to run very fast, so fast that none of the boys could catch up with me."

But, though she had no children, she knew perfectly well that the mothers at Grendel School had never had any difficulty in picking out their child from the crowd, even though they all looked much the same from a distance. Recognising someone as your very own wasn't about looks, it was about feel, and all Kitty could ever say was this: when Nicholas leaped into her arms again, on that stormy January night, she knew it was Nicholas from the feel. No, she'd never had a child, but she'd had Nicholas, and she'd loved him, and, in a funny way, "the feel" was all part of the same thing. It was about love.

Quite a long time passed before Kitty, with Nicholas in her arms, went into McGee's bedroom. McGee was snoring so heartily Kitty wondered whether she should wake her, or wait until morning. But she decided against waiting. McGee had loved Nicholas just as much as Kitty had loved him, and it was only right that she should share in the joy of his homecoming.

It took ages to wake her up, however, and only when Kitty was certain she was properly awake did she say, "McGee, I've got Nicholas. He's come back."

"*Really?*" Her friend mumbled sleepily and, before Kitty could stop him, he'd leaped from her arms and was making big muddy splodges all over Miss McGee's white counterpane.

Now McGee was a fusspot, and was very particular about cleanliness, but, do you know, she didn't turn a hair. When she was thoroughly awake she gave Nicholas a very long hug. Then she inspected him minutely, all over, for scratches and bruises, and, of course, she gave him a lot more hugs.

"I hope you're going to give this cat something to eat, Katherine Elizabeth," she said (names she only used when something really important was happening).

"Of course I am," Kitty said meekly.

"Good. Then, if you don't mind, I'll try and get back to sleep."

Now some people would have thought this was very heartless of Miss McGee. After all, Nicholas had been missing for weeks and weeks. Didn't she want to get up at once, and play with him, and marvel at his miraculous return? The answer to this question is yes, that is what she would most like to have done. But she had decided to let Kitty have some time in private with him. There was no hurry for her. With luck, Nicholas would not go missing again. There would be months, years perhaps, to enjoy his company. He'd had a big adventure and he must have been in some dangerous places. There was, for example, a piece missing out of his ear. He must surely have been in a battle!

And there was another reason why she did not get up at once and play with Nicholas, and it was this. She herself had never given up hope. She was a country person and she knew that missing cats quite often came home again, often after months and months. Cats were mysterious and wonderful creatures; she had known lots of cats. Kitty, who was a town person, had only known one.

But she had not told Kitty what she thought, because she had not wanted to raise her hopes. She had just said her prayers to St Anthony and left it with him. After all, he was the special saint for lost things. And he had answered her prayers, though in a funny, roundabout way.

Almost a year after this, Kitty stood at her window looking down into Golden Square. She could see Nicholas crouched down by the black railings, watching something very intently. As he crouched there, Fluffy came bounding along and rubbed up against him, but Nicholas took no notice. He was hunting.

He was cool towards Fluffy, and never paid him much attention. The old ladies believed this was to do with his adventure. They couldn't force him to be friendly. That was the thing about cats, you couldn't make them do anything they didn't want to.

He was a very clever cat, but he could not speak and so could never tell Kitty and Miss McGee where he had been all those long weeks when he was missing. It was, and would remain, a mystery. Why the saints Jude and Anthony had answered their prayers (or so they had thought) and sent him home, was also a mystery. Kitty thought it might be something to do with being patient, and not giving up hope, a lesson she still had to learn, perhaps, even at her age.

All the children were playing, down in Golden Square. The falling-down house had been done up in no time, by a very clever builder, and Tom the vet now lived in it with his wife and their six children, and no end of animals. Some were their own pets and some were other people's which stayed overnight, or until they got better.

Debbie's mum was working in the square again. Mrs Atkinson, had heard that she was "a treasure" and had asked her to come and help in the house. She also did some cleaning for Tom the vet and, when that cleaning was finished, she helped with the animals. Debbie came and helped too, when school was over, and she got to know Annie and Timothy Joe quite well, and all Tom the vet's six children. Now her mum came to work in the square again most days, Debbie often visited Kitty and Miss McGee, her two extra grannies. It was like old times except that it was better.

The children were throwing snowballs at one

another, and pulling each other up and down on plastic sacks, and making snowmen. One of the boys had a real toboggan.

Timothy Joe and Annie were down there, both dressed in bright red; they looked like a couple of robins. They were hurling big snowballs around with all their might. Debbie was throwing snowballs as well, but quite carefully. She was older than Annie and a lot stronger. She didn't want to hurt anyone. Annie looked plump-cheeked and rosy, it was hard to believe that she had nearly died from that terrible illness. It was a miracle. And another miracle was that it had been another, beautiful white Christmas.

And the third miracle was that Nicholas had come home.